POCKET FULL
OF POSIES

L.A. KENNEDY

A Pocket Full of Posies
ISBN # 978-1-83943-862-2
©Copyright L.A. Kennedy 2018
Cover Art by Posh Gosh ©Copyright July 2018
Interior text design by Claire Siemaszkiewicz
Totally Bound Publishing

POCKET FULL
OF POSIES

Dedication

Dedicated to Van.
Thank you for listening to the crazy.

And a huge thank you to my editor, Jamie. Thank
you for helping me get this book to where it is.

Ring-a-round the Rosie,
A pocket full of posies,
Ashes! Ashes!
We all fall down.

Chapter One

Saturday, December 7, 2013
Vancouver, Canada
Received and printed by The Vancouver Sun

Letters from a deranged mind,
Why did you not print my last letter? I found it to be elegant and honest. Was I too fucking candid? Perhaps in the way that I described how I wanted to fuck the dead man but fiddled with myself instead? I think that shows control when I could have killed his entire useless family. Did I offend your sensible fucking morals? I doubt that, given you are a newspaper and reporters lack those just like a dog lacks wings. It's what gives you the guts to photograph dead babies for ratings. I suppose you have limited options in life. You either become a journalist or you become a lawyer – then the one percent become me.

I will kill someone in your name. I will whisper your name in their ear as I carve the flesh from their twitching body. Are you happy now? Are you fucking listening now? Or do I need to sling them up in a schoolyard to let the little kiddies see what real art looks like? Not the worthless crap that the old cunts past retirement try to jam down their throats. The teachers of today are breeding the useless minds of tomorrow. Humanity is fucked, but I've got your back. Give me a few more weeks, and I'll weed them out.

Let's review the rules, shall we? When I speak, you fucking listen. When you ignore me, I will express myself through the flopped carcasses that I'll line your dirty fucking streets with. I'll nail them to your front fucking door. Do you think your bastard children would like that? Shall I give them a little lesson in etiquette, since you clearly have no idea what that is?

I am your wickedest nightmare. I am the incubus of your sanity and safety, because I know it isn't your own pain you dread the most. It is the pain of your loved ones you fear more than anything I could possibly do to you. But isn't that the crux of love? I don't feel love. I don't drink from the pool of poison, but understanding it makes my art grander. It makes those moments all the more memorable. It gives me inspiration. The brilliance is that I won't have to guess who you love. You will show me willingly without noticing I am even watching you. But I'm always watching you. You're a pawn to me, each one of you. Your worst nightmare is my most cherished dream. I savored the moments where I knew I had taken your loved ones and twisted them into the grandest of memories. Their last breaths, the very last seconds, the moments their lights go out are orgasms for my soul. Yes, I still have one of those. Can you say the same? For most of you, you're shells of what humanity was meant to be.

Vancouver is strange, but so am I and so are you. I've seen worse – worse places and worse people than you or me. I saw the inner cockles of the cesspools we call home. It makes one feel dirty just stepping off the plane, like the disgust is seeping into your pores and coating your veins with the tears of every whore who drinks down dirty men for blow. I've met folks who make you want to remove a layer of skin from just one touch. It's not just this handsome city. It's in every corner of this world. The evil you all try to ignore is like that bat-shit crazy grandmother you only bring out for Christmas – ignored until the reading of her will.

Our cities hold parts they wish to hide from the rest of the sophisticated world, spewing out of the crack-infested alleys like crawling cockroaches and beggars, cities built on broken dreams like the jagged-toothed grin of an old junkie, tucked behind the shops in places you see on commercials, holding the colorless, forbidding, grim, faded graffiti and dirty needles that will kill faster than the shit it once held.

The women pursue fresh cock in their meager outfits and boots so high they rub on their dirty cunts while they search for a new, diseased lap to spread their legs for. Their drugged-out bodies are as thin as dashes, their cheekbones jutting out through their colorless skin. They already look dead. They make my stomach roll and pinch at my sanity. The carefully constructed façade is more fragile than the glass that is blown for the tourists. Little glass balls bring the foolish downtown for the beggars and dealers to mug. The circle of life is a dirty fucker. It brought me here after all, didn't it? Maybe you can thank your God for that or Mother Nature – or whatever fucking lies you tell yourself. Add it to the other bullshit like "Daddy loves me. He isn't hurting me. He loves me."

What's oddest about Vancouver, different from other places, is the blunt truth thrust in your face the moment you step outside. There's no bullshit. Its welcome sign should read 'This is us. Don't like it? Get the fuck out.' I can respect that. But respect don't pay the bills, and it won't keep me from turning your gutters red or stringing intestines from your charming little Christmas trees. I say it would add a festive flare to the excitement of the season, but that's just me. I've waited and watched and noticed how the holidays remove basic manners and human dignity. It's made my shopping all the easier.

It is insanity out there, and it's killing you all – granted, slower than I would. We rip babies from vaginas, some to kill and some to sell for money. We devised a system that doesn't rely on mercy or true freedom or love, and you say I'm mad? I'm crazy? You created me. Mankind has built a living and breathing creature that starves children to their deaths, and I get more coverage than babies dying. We produce disease but can't afford to cure it, yet you pump money into my capture? People kill people in the name of a God because he differs from someone else's God, and you will kill me because I believe in no God? If there ever was one, he left long ago. Search around you. The only omnipotent person here is your dealer, your whore and your cell phone company, yet you look at me as though I'm evil. I'm no different from those you pay to run our countries into the fucking ground, only I don't bomb nations or kill children. Who am I kidding? If I had a bomb, I'd undoubtedly use it.

Tomorrow I will show you all what ignoring me does. I haven't yet decided if I will take the husband or the wife. Maybe I'll take both? 'Tis the season for giving, after all. The husband is a fraud and a prevaricator. His spouse is an ignorant, cock-sucking moaner. Her weeping in her car is enough to make me want to plow her into oncoming traffic – not out of hate but out of clemency. Putting that bitch out of her wretched misery would be a kindness to us all, like seeing a mangled cat on the freeway and running it over again.

The trepidation is killing me. Decisions, decisions, decisions. Do I go left or right? Do I kill for mercy or for rage? We shall see. What I know for certain is that if you keep ignoring me, you will find me on your fucking doorstep, giving candy to your spoiled-rotten children.

The newest will make a divine display of the grotesque humanity the world wades through every day. A perfect specimen, either one I select. I will wrap my hands around their snappy little throat and take away what they don't

deserve — life. I will wait in their house built of cards on a foundation of lies and bring it crumbling down around them.
   Until we meet.
   Your friend always, TNK, The Nursery Killer.

* * * *

Brock

"Hale, briefing in five." A voice pulled my attention from the article in the paper.

A budding serial killer had written to *The Vancouver Sun* and its headlines had gone worldwide. The press had coined him The Nursery Killer, TNK, glamorizing the sick fuck. Ratings meant everything nowadays. There wasn't a single officer in Canada who wasn't gunning for TNK, and every state was on the alert for the possibility of the killer jumping borders. TNK taunted them, warning them for months leading up to the murders and relishing in the fact that they hadn't caught up with him yet. The bastard was about to kill again and there wasn't a fucking thing anyone could do about it. Vancouver was on the verge of mass panic. It was a fear so great that the FBI was called in for help. TNK wasn't the first killer who had caused cities to damn near board up their windows, and he wouldn't be the last.

I pushed the printout from the newspaper to the side, downed a few antacids, grabbed my folder and headed for the door. I'd be offering up some additions to a makeshift profile on TNK, a desperate attempt at understanding the fuck who was running the streets of Vancouver. I slipped into the conference room and stood at the back. The meeting was already in full swing. I knew the drill — shut up until asked to speak.

Enough years with the FBI and I could gauge the pressure by just how many people were in attendance. Forty suits with one name and one focus—TNK.

In all my years, I hadn't ever seen horror like the carnage left behind by TNK. And I had witnessed enough shit to pour my ass into two divorces, a case of Scotch and enough hookers to keep a bottle of penicillin on standby. TNK was different. There was something about the killings that was more personal than anything I had ever seen. Days and weeks had gone into the planning of the most gruesome deaths I'd had the misfortune of seeing in all my days. At any moment, the phones would be ringing with another scene. It wasn't a matter of *if* it would happen, only *when* it would happen.

With one nod, I stood at the front and did my song and dance. I had analyzed every letter and had come up with a few details no one else had thought of. I wished I could have taken credit for it, but it had been an academy class that connected the dots. Kiss-asses, the lot of them. TNK might not even be Canadian. We could be looking for a tourist or a border jumper. Everything about the letters had suggested TNK was American. And if that were true, the FBI would be balls deep in someone else's pond, trying to clean up their little slice of home. Usually, with the prospect of jumping borders, I was pounding Advil, trying to ward off the pending headache it would bring me. Not this time. This time they wanted the FBI there, and I was thankful I wouldn't have to go. I had too many open cases on the burner, and for once, I was grateful for that.

I closed up shop and headed home. By home, I meant the pub on the corner. There's no place like home. Arnold's Pub was as close as it was going to get. My apartment was empty, not of possessions though.

My newest ex had been fair in the division of assets, but it was bare of everything that gave it a sense of home. It reminded me of what I'd lost to climb the ladder in a job that damn near killed me each day. Every case took a piece of my soul with it. Each day I walked through the front doors and faced pure evil and a small slice of my sanity was left behind at the crime scene.

The glamorous life of an agent felt like a slow drag behind a pickup truck to the loony bin if I didn't eat my gun first.

Chapter Two

Sunday, December 8, 2013, two a.m.
The Golden Mile, Point Grey, Vancouver, Canada
Residence of Dr. Henry Grant and Dr. Mary Grant
Mary

Twilight had rolled in over Point Grey, draining its color to dull oyster then nothing at all. Our piece of the world was covered with thick clouds that swallowed the day and blotted out the stars. The remaining light of the evening sky had been obliterated. It brought with it the threat of another winter storm. Winter in Vancouver was unforgiving to those who baked on the beach for three quarters of the year. The air hung icy cold and cumbersome. It could be felt in the pit of your stomach. Frosted wind howled through the trees that lined our suburban block and bit at the frozen skin of anyone who braved its touch. Vancouver seemed to lie barren and lifeless under the grip of winter. The shorter days and longer nights made us ache for summer again. It was as if God himself had put the city into a dark, cold sleep. It was the payment for the rest of the year of the welcoming sand and drinks on patios.

I liked the night. It hid the flaws, the failures and the scars that weighed on the city. The calming presence of nightfall forced me to let go of the daily baggage I carried with me from my life inside an emotional pressure tank. My mind was left open, a haze of possibilities, each more capricious than the next. That would pass when I dipped back into the tank of insanity — my job, my life's work.

"Mary, Mary, quite contrary," Henry called out to me from our four-poster bed. His voice was hoarse from him being half asleep. The nickname from childhood had stuck with me. Hearing it roll off his lips had always made me smile. His hair was still a tussled mess, a mat of tangles on the back of his head from our lovemaking.

I stood in front of the floor-to-ceiling sliding doors and peered out at the deadness of the night. A small pocket had opened in the clouds. A canopy of bright stars materialized in the ocean of blackness. The flickering reminded me of when my blood pressure dropped and my eyesight would fill with sparkles. In my line of work, my blood pressure was a constant visual amusement park. The ocean glittered, mirroring the dazzling luminescence from the restaurants and boutiques that lined the marina. Each gust of wind hammered down on the water's surface, shattering the reflection of the harbor and forcing me to blink. I could watch the ocean for hours. It was the only place in the world where life started over with every wave. The water would rise up then crash down, pulling back and out of sight. There were many times I had wished I could be like a wave and pull away the pain of life, leaving behind a new start for those who were drowning in it.

Henry ruffled the layers of blankets, covering himself in one. He stood behind me, pulled me into his warmth and looked out into the nothingness of Point Grey. Henry had all the height of a man but none of the bulk. He was perpetually eighteen, and he had stolen my heart without even knowing I had it pre-wrapped and waiting for him.

I was the second child born into the upper-class home of Mr. and Mrs. Macmillan. The teaching began at birth. My sister Faith had died of sudden infant death syndrome. I never knew her, and my parents had never displayed any photos of her. I had the best that money could buy and a nanny to keep me amused. I loved her. I still remembered her. She was the only love I'd felt as a child. If not for her, I don't believe I'd have survived childhood — not and be relatively sane. My days had been like everyone else's. I had attended school and clubs, done homework then eaten dinner with my parents — if you counted eating at the same table and watching them make phone calls or do paperwork. Each day had blended into the next, always the same. The only real conversations I remembered had been about my grades. The pressure of being above the rest was much like walking a tightrope in the middle of a hurricane. A mark less than an 'A' in any subject had meant punishment. Because of that, I had grown into a shy girl, bordering on morose. Somehow I had developed the belief that my parents had wished Faith had lived, and I was the disappointment who had died. Then I'd met Henry.

When he had taken my hand and told me I didn't need to be anyone other than who I wanted to be, he'd freed me in some way. I'd come out of the shell I'd built around me. He hadn't promised me riches or the house with a white picket fence. He'd never regaled me with money, although we both had more than we needed. And he had no plans for living a luxurious life. But he'd promised to love me, the kind of love neither of us had experienced before. It was the type of love that would put me above all else, love that could make a man charge into hell and face off against the devil himself. Soon, he and I were against the world. Our parents were long dead now, both of us only children. But we had each other, and that was more than what we'd had growing up.

I looked at the clock, almost two in the morning. "I have to go. There's an emergency at the hospital. I'm needed."

Henry kissed my shoulder. It sent tingles down my spine. "You're always needed, Mary. I thought you weren't on call this weekend?"

I turned and wrapped my arms around his shoulders, pursing my lips and scrunching my nose. "I'm not, but Dr. Waters was knocked out during an assessment and is a little shaken up."

Henry kissed my nose. "How does a child get the upper hand?"

I shrugged. "Survival instincts kick in. When you're scared, backed into a corner, alone, your natural instinct is to fight for survival. It doesn't matter how old you are. And when you've spent your little years being abused and neglected, your 'fight, flight, freeze' responses are pretty extreme. Trauma makes us all do what we need to do to survive. That and who the hell wants to take down a child and traumatize them even more?"

"I'll make you a cup of coffee to go. It sounds like you'll need it." Henry pulled away, smiling. He knew my job meant the world to me and he never once complained about it. "Don't forget that we have dinner plans tonight. If you get caught up at the hospital, I'm taking the attractive mailman with me."

I laughed. "Mr. Thompson would probably love that."

That was my Henry — supportive, funny and corny, just like me. We both worked at Vancouver General — he in pediatrics and me as a psychologist. I collaborated on a case-by-case basis with the local police, but my heart was in the hospital. Wherever we were, we were together. Some said we spent too much time together. I said they didn't know what real love was.

As tempted as I was to dress in my ugly scrubs, I wore a pantsuit and flats. I twisted my hair into a bun and grabbed my coffee in hand then I kissed Henry goodbye. By the time I got home later, he'd either have left for work or he'd be on his way out of the door. The only saving grace to being out at this hour was the traffic. Two in the morning on a Sunday had slowed the traffic into nearly nothing except shift workers and emergency vehicles. The closer I got to the hospital, the more traffic became an issue.

My locker was tucked away at the end of the blue line. I had been given it on a temporary basis since funding had been too tight to offer me a full-time position. After one year, a few extra dollars had come in, and I had been granted the title of employee and not just contracted. I unlocked it to find a small white card taped to my top shelf. It was very much like Henry to leave me little love notes. I did the same for him. Above the card was a small cluster of flowers, no bigger than a plum.

Ring-a-round the Rosie.

I flipped it over. Nothing else was written. I wondered for a moment about the meaning to the nursery rhyme. I knew it had been associated with the plague at one point. Was this doctor banter that I wasn't getting? He did have the oddest sense of humor. More times than not, the joke went over my head. I put the card up, smelled the flowers and continued about my middle-of-the-night duties. From coffee to coffee, room to room, I had managed to finish an assessment, do my morning rounds and get out of there before it was time for lunch. I took the rest of the day off. There would have been no point to me staying, not with caffeine shakes and a foggy mind.

Tonight, Henry and I had dinner plans with our closest friends, the McConnells, Calvin and Sara. They have been our closest friends since we first moved to Vancouver eight years ago. They had been our neighbors until Calvin and Sara had sold their house and relocated to the West End. I missed them. As life grew busier, I missed them less and less. But we did our best to carve out time to see each other and keep that relationship alive.

Once home, I hit the button for the garage and waited. Nothing. I grumbled and parked in our driveway. The garage had been fixed twice this year, only for it to fail again. With the weather, I half suspected it was frozen shut. That wouldn't have surprised me. On the front door, I found another white card with the same verse.

Ring-a-round the Rosie.

Frowning, I was too tired to rack my brain for the meaning. A small part of my selfishness had hoped Henry had gone to work and hadn't planned some sort of activity. I knew I couldn't have even tried to fake my way through an afternoon. I needed sleep.

I opened the door and stepped into a nightmare covered in sun rays and the yellow promise of a beautiful day. The sunlight is the same as a camera. It tells no lies and presents the world in the harshest of color. In a world that bombards you with hard reality, daylight gives it the edge that can drive a person to their knees. It shows every flaw and horror in glorious Technicolor. My senses were assaulted and shaken like a martini. I stepped into the front room, slipping and fumbling to keep my balance.

The floor was sticky wet, throwing me to my hands and knees. The floor had been painted, but the smell didn't match. I scanned our entrance, taking in the color red. The red had flowed out of a now limp and lifeless body in the middle of the room, propped up to welcome me home. Where there once had been soft and honeyed skin was now gray and ashen. Torn muscle and blood, as raw as any carcass at the butcher's, replaced Henry's once-toned body. The lips I had kissed just hours ago were ripped and still, lifeless like the rest of him. His insides were splattered onto the floor, leaving a design of intricate patterns. His milky eyes remained open, staring blankly at me, no longer brilliant blue. The air once perfumed with lavender was replaced by the smell of a meat market. The carnage had seeped into every corner. The heinousness took away the love in the home. It was ruined by the gore of the blood.

I broke inside. Like a chandelier falling onto a marble floor, my sanity shattered into a million pieces. It smashed, shimmering like crystal in the sun. Who knew breaking down could feel so beautiful? I fell to my side, knowing my mind could take no more, so I didn't even try to maintain myself. I stayed there, staring at the end of my world, whispering to myself, "I'm done." *I've reached my limit, and now I'm just done.*

The panic started in my chest. It was as if my mind was willing my muscles to not let in another breath, to suffocate me and allow me to die with my Henry. Then the breath came, shallow, just enough to keep my heart pumping. My mind became static. My thoughts made little sense. The photographs my mind had taken the moment I had stepped into my home replayed like scenes from a horror show. I remembered choking on words, trying to call for help. I could feel my mind snap some more.

They say I ran into the streets, covered in blood and screaming for help. They say I screamed about demons and evil that no one could see. I was taken to the very same hospital I had just come home from. They took away everything sharp and anything I could use to hang myself with. They didn't trust me enough to allow me to use a pen or to sign papers and they used two other doctors to do it for me. My world flashed before my eyes, playing in fast forward then slowing to a crawl. My every word was scribbled on a pad of paper. They took my statement and left me in a gown, pumped full of enough medication to take down an elephant.

If the breaking of my sanity and heart was hard to bear, the recovery from it was far worse. After finding my husband torn apart in our home, after the emergency room and the police, after the stripping me of my clothing for evidence, being stuck with drug filled needles, placed in a room with no handles and no way out, came the treatment and doctors and pills and more head shrinks. The looks of concern and pity drove me to be thankful I was unconscious through the worst of it. The drugs pushed my head into a haze where my thoughts were stagnant and my emotions were too far away to touch.

Henry had been killed at three in the morning, one hour after I had left for work. There had been no witnesses and no one had heard a thing. The card left in my locker had no fingerprints, and the security cameras hadn't caught enough for an ID. The murder went unsolved. I spent two weeks in the hospital and one month in a hotel while the house was cleaned, packed and sold. I resigned from Vancouver General and moved back to the US, back into my parent's brownstone. Both of my parents had been gone long enough for me to not feel as I had when I had been a child — an unwanted visitor.

Between my hospital stay and my move into a hotel, two more people had been killed, four in total. Each time someone was murdered, the rest of the nursery rhyme would be found on cards — four deaths, four cards, one nursery rhyme. *Ring-a-round the Rosie*. The killing ended when the verse ended. The killer was cleverly coined by the media, "The Nursery Killer". I spent the next three years immersed in serial killers and criminology.

* * * *

In December 2014, The Nursery Killer returned. This time, his body count was higher, to the tune of *Three Blind Mice*. They had all been killed within the same four-week duration in the same gruesome fashion, only this time, they were missing their eyes and one limb to signify "cut off their tails with a carving knife". Each victim had been from Fargo, North Dakota. Again, there were no leads and no suspects.

December 2015, the killer returned, leaving cards and bodies to the rhyme of *Diddle, Diddle, Dumpling, My Son John*. The killer killed four johns, and the sex trade worker found with them. The murders were gory and over the top, staged impeccably for onlookers. The killer left no trace evidence. Each victim had been from Houston, Texas. Again, the killer would leave and disappear for another year.

The heartache I had felt from losing my soul mate had wrung me out like a wet beach towel until I was dry inside. After almost three years, my heart and soul no longer felt the rawness of a sandstorm blowing through my body. My last conversation with Henry had haunted me, replaying over and over in my mind. Now I could just hear it over the sound of having to pick myself up and move on. At the start, it felt like I was dishonoring him, but I knew that is what he would have wanted. If the situation were reversed, I would want him to live—really live.

I would live—for me, for Henry. And I would do everything I could to take down the next sick fuck who tried to destroy a life.

Chapter Three

Wednesday, November 30, 2016
New York City
Received and printed by The New York Post

Letters from a deranged mind,
I think the years have broken me, removed my desire for
proper art. My revulsion in you cannot be contained. I need
the light in your cold black eyes to be extinguished. The only
saving grace is that the hate for you colors my soul. But I'm
not crazy. I'm good and sane. Why do you all look at me like
that? Like you know just how fucking cracked I can be?
Everyone is mad here. I'm not just another crazy person who
thinks bugs are crawling on their skin. The only insects I see
are you all, scurrying like maggots.
Mankind — or what is left of it — scratches at my brain and
brings a twitch to my eye. The stench in the streets brings
out the rats to feed on the death the world ignores. I often
walk the streets, eyeing the passersby, wondering what their
sin buckets hold. I watch parents and their screaming
children walk up and down the blocks. What I wouldn't give

to grab on to a child and let them know that it's only going to get worse. Their little temper tantrums over inconsequential bullshit is nothing compared to what life will do to them as they age. Each block of the septic system called mankind contains rape, incest, infidelity, murder, setting cats on fire, theft, suicide and worse. Not a single grain of sand in the world has gone untouched by mankind with hateful verbal vomit.

You all have such lovely smiles. Your lips are perfect, moist and supple. I like your lips. I want to carve each one off and put them in a tin to save for later, to build a collection. Have you seen my tin? It's small, silver and smells of death, just like your back alleys and whores on the corner.

Why do you not talk to me? You're not very nice. None of you are that fucking special either. You're not very social. Why do you all walk away from me when I try to talk to you?

Why must you fucking walk away from me?

I see you all on Friday nights with your polished hair done up and your makeup expertly applied. It makes you appear beautiful, like the whore your daddy calls you. I wish I could pull the hair from your head – flesh attached – and save it with your lips. I hate you. You're a bitch. When I call you a whore, you make a twisted face at me. I want to save that face, sliced exactly how it is, roll it up and put it in my tin. Have you seen my tin? Why must you all look at me like that? Why can't you just be nice?

I hate the smell of blood and gore. It turns my stomach. It makes me puke hard enough to almost piss my pants. But your blood makes my body twitch. It makes me want to come all over it, mixing me and you together. I want to rub myself with your blood. In the darkness, the blood blends with your exquisite hair. It colors your already-red lips. I'd like you covered in your own filth because you know you're filthy. You're a rat, an infected rodent. You should be set on fire with the rest of the creeps in the sewers.

Never mind. Call off the search. I've found my pretty tin. That was a close one. Fuck, I can be pretty forgetful sometimes. Paint me silly.

New York, New York!

Hello, New York, I'm happy to be here. You remain exactly how I remembered you, devoid of humanity and warmth. You are a collection of buildings and bodies. Your roads are like torn, pay-by-the-hour hotel carpet. The only real sound here comes from the hooker who wants to suck you down for a bump of blow or the hobo who tells you he is starving. If I stand still long enough, I can feel you scratching at my bones and lucidity. I won't be here long. One month, perhaps. I came to visit some old friends. You should pray we do not know each other or I may be knocking on your door next, and you will let me in. You always do. I am a wolf among sheep.

I'm glad you're printing my letters. I feared I'd have to do a door-to-door campaign, personally convincing each of you of the importance of not ignoring me. You're much politer than Vancouver was. That's a high compliment coming from me, considering I wouldn't piss on a single one of you if you were on fire. I'll put my can of gasoline away for now. But rest assured, if one letter goes unpublished, the city will need some marshmallows.

Until we meet.

Your friend always, TNK

* * * *

Brock

A few months ago, I had thought my transfer to New York was the worst thing to have happened to me. I had sworn it was a punishment for me wanting to eat my gun at my lowest point, sort of a slap in the face, really.

Twenty-six Federal Plaza, Twenty-third floor, Manhattan was my new stomping grounds. I wasn't a fan of the location, but I didn't hate it. It was a step up of sorts for my career. But I was leaving everything I knew, everyone I had known, behind. Change was something that didn't come easy for me. Drowning my sorrows in another version of home, Sal's Bar, a dive that smelled worse than city cells, was where I ended my nights. I would drink until the broken pieces inside me would pass out from the fiery booze. We're all a little broken inside, I suppose. Most of us carry layers of tape and glue, holding our souls together. I was no different. Years of hell had taught me a thing or two. Nothing lasts forever, and it can always get worse. I was always waiting for the worst to come or my life to end. In my line of work, that's pretty much a given, the only guarantee.

That was until *she* walked into my home away from home.

She stepped into Sal's with the winter snow billowing in behind her. Sal's had just over thirty diehard boozehounds and most didn't pay any mind to her beauty, not in the way I had. She wasn't beautiful in a conventional way — no flowing stripper blonde hair or golden curls, no piercing eyes or winter vacation tan. She was average height and larger than a catwalk model, but in her ordinariness, she was magnificent. Something radiated from within her that rendered her irresistible.

She moved through the bar with an effortless saunter. Her shoes clicked on the sticky, booze-soaked floor, adding a soft rhythm to the blues music playing in the background. She scanned the room, not looking for anyone in particular but for someone for the night. I knew that expression. I *had* it. When her eyes met mine, she smiled in acknowledgment of my staring at her. That smile... That was what did it for me. It was like the gods themselves had paid particular attention to her mouth. My cock twitched with just one smile. I prayed she would sit close enough for me to get another.

"Is this seat taken?" she asked.

"Not at all," I replied. Hell, I'd have pulled a gun on the shmuck who claimed that chair, just so she'd sit next to me.

She removed her woolen knee-length jacket, and I almost fell off my seat. Her black-on-black suit had a tailored look that was bold against the paleness of her skin. I could almost envision her naked, leaned back with her thighs wide open and her greedy pussy begging for me. The suit hugged every curve and left little to the imagination. The woman that took a seat next to me would be the woman I would stroke myself to later. The very thought of it had tested the strength of my zipper. My cock pulsed with almost enough force to rip denim for a taste of freedom.

Two drinks in and we were talking. Starting a conversation with a complete stranger — attractive or not — was one of my greatest assets. I wouldn't be good at what I did if I couldn't pluck a random conversation out of my ass. The woman was oblivious to her beauty. And with every additional drink, her once-flawless skin showed the same lines around her eyes that I had. Below all the beauty, she was broken somehow, as was I. Perhaps, like me, she had been robbed of the tape and glue we all used to keep our shit together. And even with that knowledge of her brokenness, I couldn't tear myself away from her. It reminded me of how desperate I was for the human connection we all craved. I'd never admit it out loud, but I more than desired connection. I was starved for it.

I'd learned years ago that I was shattered inside. My heart, poorly stapled shut, was beating without much purpose. It was tedious. Find a body, interview the family, locate the killer... It was oftentimes someone who'd sworn to protect them. Case closed and on to the next horrifying body. My mind was no more than a drowning man's at sea, desperate for a reason to live — not just exist but truly live. After my first marriage, I couldn't remember the last time I had smiled a real, genuine smile. Something that comes from within and turns your eyes into crescent moons. Not since the first day I had stepped into my first office had I smiled that way. Sad, but true, that the first thrill of the hunt had made me smile wider than my first love. My soul had grown greedy for whatever it could get. I had told myself that each cunt I crawled into was healing my heart, but it knew it was nothing more than destruction.

Years of work and a transfer had gotten me to a place where I was able to accept why I was broken. A childhood that made a cult seem like Mr. Rogers' neighborhood had been the start of my journey. My mother, a soul finally at peace, had been a crack addict who loved to sell her children to whack jobs for a few rocks and a clean spoon. My father, whoever he was, hadn't stuck around long after he'd introduced my mother to the wonderful world of poor man's ecstasy and a one-up of a crack whore. From state home to state home, I'd gotten a lovely little taste of what it meant to be a meal ticket. Bruised and battered, I'd made my way to adulthood with a chip on my shoulder.

I shook all thoughts of the train from hell from my mind and focused on the reason my pulse was speeding beside me. The woman turned, holding all the charm of the bar in her eyes. She moved close enough that I could feel her warm breath on my face. She spoke just four words.

"Your place or mine?"

"My name is Brock... Brock..." I started, finally realizing we hadn't exchanged names.

"No, no last names. I don't need it. That just complicates things. Call me Mary," she replied. She ran her tongue over the rim of my ear and placed a kiss on my throat. "Your place or mine?

"Mine," I responded. "It's just around the corner."

* * * *

Stretched out on my mattress, the bedding half on and half off the bed, I watched her. She stood at the foot, the woman who made every inch of my body tremble. I couldn't take my eyes off her. From head to toe, I wanted all of her in my mouth. She was a masterpiece, and I pulled her to me. Her taste was like putting a firecracker in my mouth and closing my lips. It ignited every one of my senses and pulled my brain out of its booze-soaked slumber. Every nerve twitched. I couldn't get enough of her soft skin and needed every piece of my body touching hers.

Mary fisted my hair and ground against my mouth. When I could tell her orgasm was approaching, I climbed up her body and pushed myself inside her welcoming pussy. I focused on bringing her orgasm and fought with all my might not to come before her. She dug her nails into my arms and screamed my name. The sound of my hips colliding with her thighs filled the room. I hooked my arms under hers and fucked her until my balls tightened.

"Come for me," she groaned from beneath me.

Those three words sent my brain into overdrive. I came hard and fast and felt like I was about to fall off the edge of the world. I couldn't remember the last time I'd had an orgasm that felt half as good as the one I had just experienced.

In my arms I held a woman I hadn't known yesterday but felt like I had known all my life. Every curve of her body fit snug alongside mine as though we had been made for each other. She was caged madness for me. I hadn't felt this alive or this needed and wanted for so long that I had convinced myself I had never felt it before. Once I'd pushed myself into her wetness and her body had gripped around mine, I knew I had finally found a home deep inside her.

That was the first of many nights we shared. We would meet at the bar then spend hours with me buried inside her. We exchanged very little in the form of words, aside from animalistic groans and pleading for the next orgasm. After several weeks, I didn't regret my move to New York.

Special Agent in Charge of the high-profile case, TNK... That was me. Assistant Director in Charge Franklyn had handed over the case. This was my shot. My one chance to show them what I've got, and I was damn excited. With the file came a list of names and one psychologist who knew the mind of a killer, inside and out. I opened the file and choked on my coffee.

Dr. Mary Grant, wife of victim Dr. Henry Grant. I had to read it several times and look at her photo over and over before it hit me. The Mary I had been sleeping with was the wife of a victim and I had to go to her and ask for help. If this wasn't the very definition of heartbreakingly awkward, I didn't know what was.

The FBI had worked to stop TNK letters from being published, an effort to take back control. No court would order an injunction, claiming First Amendment rights. It was a media shit storm with speculation and city-wide panic threatening to spill into the streets. With another letter released to the press, I stood in the hall of NYU. I would have given my left nut to be somewhere else. But another part of me, the part that cared for a woman I had known nothing about, had wanted to be the one to comfort her. I needed my own head doc to explain to me why I felt I owed my repeated one-night stand an explanation. She hadn't offered up any information about who she was. Why did I feel like I had screwed her over?

Professor McNally, a close friend of Dr. Mary Grant, paced the hallway in front of the lecture hall. "She isn't going to like being interrupted. Can this not wait until after her class?"

"Respectfully, no. I mentioned on the telephone that this is of high importance," I responded.

"Why must you bring her into this? Hasn't she suffered enough?" he asked me, and he was right.

Personally, I didn't really want to be there. It killed me inside to know I'd be bringing Mary back to a place of pain. But, professionally, I knew she was the best, and we needed the best. I'd do just about anything to keep another person from being in her position, rebuilding after horror. I couldn't stop the little voice in the back of my mind from jumping to all sorts of conclusions. *Will she hate me for this? Will she call me out in front of the others? Does it really matter?* Everyone had already thought I was nothing more than a womanizer, anyway. I had earned the nicknames — gigolo, Romeo and my personal favorite, Don Juan the Letch. The crueler of the terms were from the ladies who I had fucked over, both figuratively and physically.

Professor McNally opened the door to the auditorium. I caught a glimpse of Mary and my stomach flopped, landing in the toes of my shoes. What pet name would she call me after I turned her life upside down and stomped on any resemblance of the one that she had built since her encounter with TNK? I wanted to turn around and run for the hills. I didn't want to face her. I began to mentally kick my ass for not talking to her beforehand. I'd had nothing but opportunity. Instead, I'd stopped meeting up with her at Sal's. I hadn't been able to face her then, either.

Chapter Four

Wednesday, November 30, 2016 – six p.m.
6 Washington Place, Room 970
New York University, New York
Dr. Mary Grant, Forensic Psychology Lecture
Mary

Over the speakers I played a recording from a budding serial killer I had interviewed the previous year. There was something about the girl I interviewed that had made my skin crawl more than any other I had assessed.

"Everyone says I'm evil. I don't think I'm wicked, but I know I'm not a good girl – not in the ways that it matters to people like you. I just think what makes me tick is wired differently than with you. Most people will look at a kitten and see a cute and fuzzy creature, something to cuddle and love, like a baby. I see something I can kill. I don't want to just kill it, though. I want to see how long it can last while I eviscerate it, slowly and methodically, taking notes. I need to see the light go out in its eyes while I play with its innards."

"Why?" I asked.

"I could say I did it for scientific purposes because I was a science geek, but that would be a blatant lie. The truth is, I relish it. I get a thrill from it. I record my sessions, just like you do. Only I do it so I could play it over and over to relive the moment while I play with myself. Do you play with yourself when you listen to your sessions?"

"No, I do not," I answered.

"Liar. Be glad they were just kittens and squirrels. Soon, when you have no choice but to release me, I'll graduate to bigger and better. It will be fucking glorious. In some cultures a girl like me would be valued. We'd be respected. Perhaps I'll move away, start over, where no one knows my name. Or maybe I'll stay here and make sure you all never forget it."

I turned off the recording. "Myth One. All serial killers are males between the ages of thirty-five and forty-five. Anna was fourteen when I interviewed her. She had been responsible for setting fires, killing neighborhood pets and petty crimes. She was an only child, parents not divorced and she had the highest IQ in the state. There were no child welfare complaints, and to our knowledge, she was not a victim of child abuse or neglect. Her family attended church but were not overly religious. They were a middle class, working family. She had adequate supervision, no corporal punishments such as whipping or spanking. She was a typical girl with a small social circle — until she attempted to kill two of her friends. She administered a sleeping medication to both of them, restrained them and proceeded to strangle them then revive them. She continued this for twenty-seven hours. She was captured when neighbors heard loud music and called in a noise complaint. Capturing her was a complete fluke."

I stood from my seat in front of the classroom. All those sets of eyes would be on me. The topic was Serial Murderers. I was giving a lecture on profiling, a favor for a colleague, Professor McNally. I had spent the year touring police stations and schools, picking apart profiles of serial killers, to get to the guts of them. Today we were looking at the myths behind serial killers. The very act of stepping up onto the stage had made my breathing rapid. My pulse had pounded in my temples. It was a relief to make it to the podium. Between the heels I wore and my legs shaking, I'd feared that I'd fall flat on my face.

The inky darkness submerged the room, diminishing the anxiety that had risen the moment I'd stood from my seat. Now only silence lingered in the air, hanging on my will to open my mouth. The room, which held over two hundred people, felt like a claustrophobic cubicle. The students waited for my signal, but a small sigh of anxiety leaped out of my mouth first. The dimness of the room helped calm me. I could feel the eyes on me, but I couldn't see them. It allowed me to lie to myself. Even after the passing years, public speaking was not my strength. I took another deep breath and clicked on the projector to slide one.

On the overhead was one sentence.

Serial killers usually do not travel interstate or long distances in search of victims.

"Myth Two. On the rare occasion that this does occur, it can typically be attributed to one of several factors — military or work related, they are fleeing capture or justice, expanding their comfort zone or an increase in confidence or they are simply drifters, homeless or loners."

I clicked the slide on the overhead.

"Myth Three. Serial killers are insane evil geniuses. I won't say that someone with genius level IQ will not become a killer or that they won't go mad, but I am saying that serial killers are often suffering from personality and other behavioral disorders. They are logical and methodical in their approach. And like any other activity you work at, they tend to improve their skills and avoid detection. That really has little to do with being geniuses."

I changed the slide. I was surprised that no one in the class had raised their hand yet to ask about Henry or The Nursery Killer. Typically, after a few minutes, I had a slew of questions to avoid — or at least a wannabe FBI behavioral asking a dozen questions at once.

"Myth Four. Serial killers want to be caught. No, plain and simple. Contrary to popular belief, they do *not* want to get caught. They take great care in ensuring they avoid detection to continue for as long as possible. It is usually negligence on their part that leads to their capture. Many people believe that serial killers are always caught while in the midst of a killing frenzy. That is rarely the case. I won't say there isn't a small percentage that are in it for the fame and glory, but typically that isn't what we find."

Again, no questions. I scanned the room and waited. No one raised a hand. I clicked to another slide.

"Myth Five. Signatures. Signatures are a rare phenomenon, contrary to popular belief. The media tends to popularize this aspect of serial murder — "

"What about Jack the Ripper? Didn't he coin his own name?" a young man called out from the crowd.

This one always came up. People tended to believe everything they saw in a movie, as though the film was nothing but fact.

"No, the offender did not. First, this killer was never captured. We can hazard a guess about the sex of the offender, however, we cannot say for certain if they were a male or female. We can *never* say for certain, until they are captured. To answer your question, in 1931, a journalist reportedly confessed that he and a colleague from *The Star* had written the letters and signed the name 'Jack the Ripper' to intensify interest in the murders and to launch the circulation of the newspaper sky-high."

The auditorium door opened at the rear left. A sliver of light pierced the room and brought all of our attention to the back of the auditorium. Three men dressed in black suits with black trench coats stepped in. They didn't stick out at all.

"Myth Six. Serial killers are motivated by sex. This is not true for all. There are many driving forces for an offender. Lust, greed, personal gain, thrill, attention-seeking behavior, anger, revenge, replaying childhood trauma... All of these can be motivation in an offender's repertoire."

The overhead lights slowly lit up. Professor McNally stood at the top of the stairs with the three men in suits. He motioned for me to join him.

"April, if you could take over for a moment?" I turned to my assistant. April Norris, Ph.D. student and assistant extraordinaire, jumped from her seat and took my place in front of the podium and clicked another slide. She knew the material inside and out.

"Distinguishing an MO from a signature..." April spoke, not skipping a beat.

I stepped off the stage and made my way to the professor. I could feel the eyes on me, like little ants marching on my shoulders.

"Dr. Mary Grant?" Suit One asked and extend his hand. "I'm Special Agent Brock Hale."

I shook his hand and glared. I knew who he was, yet had never known he was FBI. I dropped the scowl. I couldn't blame him if I didn't ask for particulars before I climbed onto his hips. I had met him just as dirty barroom floors had become familiar to me. The smell of stale beer, vomit and cigarettes had become the end-of-my-day perfume, mixed with the stench of bad decisions. Several months ago, I'd met Brock. I hadn't even known what his last name was. I hadn't cared. Surely that was the least of my wrong-decision worries. *Brock Hall, FBI. Fuck.*

"Is there something I can do for you? Can this not wait until after my lecture?" I asked and turned my eyes away from Brock but felt the heat of his stare.

"No, this cannot wait," he replied. He motioned to the two men with him. "This is Special Agent Morgan Ridley and Special Agent Cole Nelson."

"What can I do for you?" I asked. I sounded impatient. I was beginning to fidget.

"If we could step outside, ma'am?" Special Agent Brock Hale asked with a slight twitch of a smile starting the moment he had called me 'ma'am'. That was not the last thing he'd called me, if memory served.

"Before I walk away from my class, I'd like to know what this is about." I sounded demanding, stern, a defense against the weakness I still carried around with me from wounds that have not yet healed from my childhood.

Hale leaned into my ear and whispered. At first, I thought he was going to mention the few dozen times he had been in my pants. Instead, the day I'd dreaded was here.

"The Nursery Killer."

I paused, staring at him, as though he had just said the earth and the sun were about to collide and we were all doomed. The door opened once more and I was led out of the room, which had fallen into a hush. I leaned against the hallway wall that was littered with notes about tutoring and random crap for sale. I could feel the layers of staples digging into my back through my white silk dress shirt. That little shred of discomfort kept me from pulling away and locking myself behind a brick wall in my mind.

I watched Professor McNally's lips move several times before I heard him speak. "Do you want some water or a cup of coffee?"

I nodded. The tension in my muscles made me feel more like a mannequin than a woman of flesh and bone. I wanted to melt into the wall and drift away from the words "The Nursery Killer". Yet my brain in its stupidity tried to organize the chaotic thoughts of this moment. Of course, that task was pointless. The horror that had made up my life until this moment was far too horrendous for my brain to take in the billions of factors that had come together to form just one day in my life. My nails, which were already bitten to the quick, were back under the crunch of my teeth while I strained to make sense of this. I nibbled at their frayed edges like a starved mouse. My surroundings were gone and my vision tunneled.

I hadn't noticed Professor McNally walk away, returning with a mug of hot coffee. It was my go-to drink nowadays and was much better than my first choice, vodka. The very thought of the liquid stress reliever made my fingers tingle up to my top knuckles and my throat dried. It didn't even have to touch my lips for my brain to giggle in excitement. My mind couldn't wait for the fuzziness to take over, pushing out the memories. The numbness was momentary and not nearly as lasting as therapy. Though my brain already knew all of this, it still struggled to remain stubborn in its failed attempts to protect me, to ensure my survival. What I needed for survival was the same dead sleep I gained from a bottle of vodka. But for a truly deep sleep to happen, one where I didn't wake up screaming Henry's name, I would need to be out cold before my head hit the pillow or I'd relive that moment I'd stepped into my nightmare. Not even two bottles of vodka downed could pull that off.

Like pale starfish, my hands spread around my blistering hot coffee cup. They felt frozen to the marrow. The cold caused by fear resisted the warmth that struggled to bleed in. I must've looked like a deer caught in the headlights — scared, skittish, with my mind struggling to decide between fight, flight or freeze.

"Dr. Grant?" Professor McNally called my name. I had the vague impression he had been calling out to me repeatedly.

I blinked out of my tunnel vision to focus on his face. "Yes."

"Do you want to sit?" he asked.

"No, I'm all right. Sorry," I said and peered at the agents. "What can I do for you?"

Special Agent Brock Hale — Hale, he now requested to be called — ran his hand through his black hair. He had the looks that stopped a woman in their tracks — attractive, commanding and with a gaze that could make a person squirm. My libido remembered just how squirmy a woman could be once caught in his sight. I was betting that he was batting a perfect score when it came to interrogation. From the moment I'd met him, the weight of his presence made me rack my brain for the recipe for the secret sauce and agree to anything he wanted. In his defense, I'd wanted it as badly as he had.

"I apologize for your apparent discomfort, Dr. Grant," Hale started. He didn't look apologetic. He appeared uncomfortable. Between knowing me intimately and my survivor emotion, he seemed twitchy with uneasiness. Like most people on this side of crime, being with a real person and real emotion didn't let him consider this as a number or a file. "We were told you could help us with a case."

"The Nursery Killer?" I asked. "What more can I add that I haven't already told you all? I've given my statement a dozen times."

His partner Special Agent Morgan Ridley, who was a slightly bigger man, same hair, same good looks with a scar on his chin, lifted a file. "We have a profile we would like you to review."

My eyes widened. "On The Nursery Killer?"

He nodded. "The TNK file and the profile. We understand this may be difficult for you. We've redacted the information regarding your husband, Henry."

My thoughts began to accelerate, bouncing off each other. The big bang was happening between my temples. I tried to will it to slow so I could breathe. My breaths came in gasps. I was sure I was about to black out. My heart hammered like it belonged to a group of rabbits on meth. The hall spun and I leaned over in an attempt at making the world slow to something my mind and body could manage. I felt sick. I wanted to ask someone to call nine-one-one. I thought about making the call myself, but my cell phone was in my bag in the auditorium. It was too far away. The world was moving too fast. My heart hammered like my brain was demanding the expenditure of an athlete in a race. When I finally could command my limbs to listen, I sat. Involuntarily, I began rocking, rocking, rocking. My movements became faster and jerky until I exploded into rambling.

My words were crowded and unstructured like I didn't have enough time to say what I needed to say. My sentences were fragments of thoughts that were fuzzy. All my fears tumbled out unchecked in some sort of psychological free fall. My fists were white-knuckled and gripped onto my sweater. I fell to my side, unable to breathe. The Nursery Killer was back in my life, back to haunt me, back to reduce me to a rambling idiot. *Call an ambulance… I can't breathe… He's gone… He's dead… Gone, dead, blood, dead…blackness.* And to make matters worse, the man trying to comfort me had known me in a way that my husband had. Deep breathing didn't work.

I'm gone, pulled into the darkness of safety.

Chapter Five

Mary

The panic attack had been one of the most severe I'd experienced since Henry had been taken from me. I woke up in the university staff room and was helped home by my assistant, April. The FBI had left behind three bankers boxes, the files from The Nursery Killer, along with Hale's business card. At first I had requested they be returned to Hale. It was off-cuff comments from April that had made me keep them.

She'd said, "Fear is part of being human. It's the precursor to courage. We need it, in all of its gut-wrenching terror. It forces us to wake up and do what needs to be done. Don't let fear own you. Feel it, possess it and let it be the catalyst that drives you to make sure another wife is not sitting where you're sitting, mourning the loss of her family. Or, cower from it. Let this monster take your life from you, over and over and over again. This is your choice. You can't blame a killer for the decisions you make, Mary."

My fear had always sat ready and waiting for the perfect moment to stand up and say "Remember me?" It slowly eroded the person I was born to be, the person Henry had helped me build from scratch. What had started as a contortion of my mind had become a feeling of being smothered by a pillow. I'd always fought it. Each time I woke up holding my chest I knew I was stronger because of it. I'd learned different ways to cope and manage. I relearned triggers and reconstructed the weaker parts of my sanity. Part of my recovery was giving the fear a name—a crown, if you will. I call my fear "The Nursery Killer" and now I must press against it, removing my cowardice. Naming my fear after TNK gave me a target, someone to blame for my rage.

Until now, I hadn't been willing to come face to face with my crowned fears. Sitting at my kitchen table, three bankers boxes sitting on top, I was ready. My apprehension remained tight in my chest like a fist around my lungs. I placed the profile file in front of me and stared at it. I had dimmed the lights to take away the color and realness of the photographs and papers. It allowed me to lie to myself, just enough to take the horror from the pages but not enough for me to pretend I wasn't looking at a crime scene.

It was another squally night, cold to chill to the bone, and I was reminded of the last night I'd seen Henry alive. *Who am I kidding?* Everything reminded me of Henry, including Brock Hale. With shaking fingers, I opened the file. I started with the newspaper letters. The offender taunted the police and cities with open letters to each major newspaper in the city they were tormenting. I read the letter from the day before Henry's murder and my stomach rolled with anger. Each letter after that was stranger and uglier than the last. I pushed them aside and moved on to the profile.

The Nursery Killer Profile

Victimology — Adult between the ages of nineteen and fifty-eight, no preference to sex or ethnicities, adults from all socioeconomic backgrounds, completed in areas where surveillance is lacking

Past Criminal Behavior — Prior criminal record unassociated with this crime

Precipitating Events — Abandonment by mother or wife, psychotic break due, revisiting his childhood traumas, sudden unexplained urges to kill, opportunity and means to abduct or lure victims

Offender Demographic — Older white male, forty-five to sixty-five years old, no outstanding physical features, medium in stature, harmless appearance, soft-spoken, highly educated, blue collar, transient lifestyle, no permanent residency, divorced or separated, no close family ties, no interpersonal relationships, no community ties, unremarkable and does not stand out in community, possible failed military career

Offender's Background — Childhood trauma and abuse, unstructured childhood, loss of one or both parents, feelings of abandonment, no childhood position emotional bonds, above-average education, multiple unsuccessful relationships throughout adulthood, substance abuse, previous mental health history, possible institutionalizations. Suffers from — antisocial disorder, narcissism, is a sadist and a sociopath

Details of the Crime — Location and tools are prepared before the attack. The victim is chosen and observed prior. Once in location, the victim is subdued, stripped of clothing, restrained for the purpose of sadistic torture. Victims are castrated, genitals and limbs removed, internal organs removed, strangled, left to bleed to death. Once the victim is dead, the offender will carve the body and leave in a posed position. The remaining body parts will be further dismembered and discarded. The offender does not exit the location with the victim's body parts.

I made notes while I read, separating myself from my emotions, pushing the last few tugging and guilty memories of Hale from my mind. The profile was vague, no more effective than throwing out a net and bringing in hundreds of fish when you were searching for the one with a spot on the left fin. The victimology covered any adult with any background, all races and all economic statuses. The offender was much the same — white male adult. Something itched at the back of my mind. I wasn't ready to rule out a female perpetrator, not yet.

I opened the first box and shut it right away, breathed in through my nose then out of my mouth. Even with the dim lights, the photos were too real. I calmed my pounding heart and tried again. Each photo was more gruesome than the last. By the time each victim was found, their flesh — or what was left of it — was already as cold as the frosted month they'd died in. Taking in every detail, I knew the evidence we needed was sitting amid the white earth. If not evidence, every scene told a story. I needed that story.

Three years — 2013, 2014, 2015. December 1, 2016, was mere hours away. I looked at the clock, almost midnight. Dread set in. It pushed against me with an invisible force. It locked my stomach and tempted it to evacuate my entire day. For the briefest of moments, it felt like rigor bolting my jaw and clamping my teeth shut. I breathed deeply and force it out. *It will not own me.* I knew this day would come. I pulled out Hale's business card and dialed his number.

"Hale," he answered on the second ring.

"I apologize for the late call, Special Agent Hale. This is Dr. Grant. Do you have a moment?" I asked. I stuck to our last names—professionalism over facing the obvious. I had whored around, and now it was nipping at my ass like a starved dog.

I had known the first night with Brock that sitting next to him at Sal's would burn my backside. But I more thought I'd pick up some nasty infection that required a round of antibiotics, not this. Never in a million years did I think I'd come face to face with my nightmare and him being the one to deliver it. Being just Mary to him gave me an escape from reality that knocked me down each chance it got. Being someone else gave me strength to face who I really was—a survivor, a sad and lonely widow. It also gave me hope that I could become whole again. I could trust not just another man but trust in my needs.

I heard him moving in bed and the faintest sound of a lamp clicking on. "Of course, Dr. Grant," he said with sarcasm. He caught my need to remove the personalization between us. "Did you get the files?"

"Yes, I did. I've briefly reviewed the profile and the data. There are a few problems here that I've noticed, just from a quick study."

He interrupted. "Can you be more specific?"

I rolled my eyes and shook my head. That one comment reminded me of the little I knew of Hale. Shoots from the hip, no wasting time and no bullshit... He was the type to be in your face. It was nothing like the man I had made love with countless nights. The very thought of our time together sent a shiver up my spine. I shut down my libido and focused. "If you can go a moment without interrupting me, I can be as specific as you'd like."

I could almost hear him chuckle. "My apologies, Dr. Grant. Continue."

"First, the profile has pointed to half the men in the city. If you release this profile, it's going to cause mass panic. You'll have neighbors calling the police on neighbors, police lines eaten up by reports of 'The Nursery Killer is my dad' and people pegging this on their hated friends—in short, tax dollars flushed down the toilet. I want to catch the offender as badly as the next person, given my personal stake in the matter, but this profile is crap. It looks a lot like a standard profile done by any random criminology student. Did you guys farm this out? I hope you saved your receipt."

"*I* wrote the profile, Dr. Grant," he said, obviously insulted. "Where exactly was I wrong?"

"I'm not saying you're wrong. I'm saying it's too vague. It's so ambiguous that it blankets half of the city. You need someone to rework your profile, starting from scratch. I can suggest several people who are experts at that."

"Are you free to meet tomorrow?" he asked.

"What? Why?" I couldn't keep the surprise from my voice. My heart began to pound. I bit my tongue for a moment before I damn near shouted out in delight. Yes, I wanted to see him, but it wasn't a good idea—not now. "I don't think that is a wise decision, Agent Hale. We should keep this professional."

He laughed again. I missed that laugh and scolded myself for thinking that way of him. He was a handsome man, but it was his laughter that brought me back to Sal's Bar to meet him again and again. That and the way he touched me, not just sexually. He had this way of reaching inside and caressing my brokenness.

"Although I've had some fantastic nights with you, I'm wondering if you can help us un-vague the profile," he said.

I groaned and chose to ignore his one comment. "Un-vague? Is that even a word?"

"I don't have my dictionary open at the moment," he countered with a touch of humor. "Dr. Grant, are you free for a profiling meeting?"

I paused. *Do I want to be involved? Not a chance. Should I be working with a man who I've treated as a punch card at my local gym? Nope. Is it my duty? I did my duty three years ago. Shit. Fuck.* I knew I wouldn't say no. *Is it morbid curiosity or me feeling like I have to do something to save myself from the shitty pit I've lived in since Henry? Will this give me closure? Probably not. This will be the catalyst to my final meltdown.*

"I can meet you, where and when?" I asked then added, "Hale, why are you in on this case? Did you know who I was?" No sooner had the question come out than I realized that I was scared to hear the truth.

"Not until a couple of weeks ago. It's why I stopped showing up at Sal's Bar. I apologize. I didn't know," he answered. "Perhaps when this is over, we can go for a drink and talk about it? I don't want to stop seeing you. And before you say otherwise, it wasn't just the sex that I enjoyed. I came back each time because I wanted to see you, to be with you in all ways."

That was something, I supposed. When I hadn't seen Hale around, I had thought he'd lost interest. "Strictly professional… That's the only way this can work. After this is over, we can grab a drink and talk about it. I can't promise anything, Hale. Now you know why I made it clear from the start that I didn't want anything more than a few nights with you. I don't think I can handle more than that, and I certainly don't have much to give of myself."

"I'll take it. I'll take whatever you can give, Mary." He cleared his throat. "It'll be professional from here on out, Dr. Grant. Watch your back. We have reason to believe he will strike here next. Tire tracks were left at the last scene."

"I read the tires were standard, very common. What wasn't in the file?" I asked, irritated they would leave out information.

"A herbaceous plant, found only in New York, was discovered in the soil under the tire imprints," he answered.

"You don't think I should know about this, given you have come to me for help? How do I assist you if you leave out pertinent information?" I asked. My voice was clipped and angry.

"You will see everything tomorrow, Dr. Grant, and thank you. Noon at One Police Plaza. We've set up our station there, rather than at HQ. The locals are blowing a fit that we're in their pond. This was easier than splitting up forces. Do you know where that is?"

"Yes. I will see you then," I answered and hung up.

I didn't feel the need to review any more of the information. If the FBI was leaving out chunks, reviewing what I had would be useless. I put everything away and placed it by my front door. I rechecked my security system and all my windows then made my journey up to bed. This was my least favorite part of the day, tossing and turning and trying to sleep, haunted by images I couldn't seem to forget. They hadn't grown duller over the years—instead, more brilliant. Each image was worse than the last.

I dreamed of playing poker with the devil. The winner got Henry's soul. The devil—Satan—was dressed in a red suit, dripping with blood. His red tie was a scream of swirling blood and little souls reaching out for rescue. I was not there for them. I was there for Henry only. Satan dealt the cards with a handsome grin. The corners of his mouth were torn, exposing rotting and sharp teeth.

"Mary, Mary, quite contrary. You can't win against the creator of sin," Satan spoke, looking at his five cards.

I lifted mine. They weren't perfect, but I was a damn fine poker player, thanks to a nanny with a gambling addiction. I held two queens, two aces and a two. I threw out the two and received another two. I tried not to react. Another round and I picked up a three. The Devil had not thrown a single card, as though he'd already won in his mind. My last throw, I got a queen. My heart pounded. I lay down my cards and the devil laughed in delight. He set down aces over kings. The room spun. I was now sitting in the doorway of my old house and Henry was splayed before me. The devil leaned over Henry and grabbed him by the scruff of the loose flesh at this throat.

The ringing pulled me out of my dream. Instant panic was replaced by relief and thankfulness. Being woken in the middle of the night wasn't a pain to me. It was a life raft in my sea of torment.

"Hello?" I mumbled. I was still shaking from the scream trapped in my throat.

"Mary?" Hale called out my name as I struggled to catch my breath. "Dr. Grant?"

"Yes?" I asked.

"Hale here. TNK has begun. Are you able to come to the scene?" Hale asked. He sounded hopeful but guilty for asking.

"Sorry. Can you repeat yourself?" I asked, his words echoing in my ears, my brain trying to net them in.

"The Nursery Killer... It's starting again. I'm at the scene down in Hells Gate. His calling card was left behind on the vic. Can you come take a look? There's an officer already outside your house, waiting for you."

"What? Why would you send an officer to *my* house?" I sat up, slapping the button on my nightstand, bringing the room to instant light. "You knew I wouldn't say no, didn't you?"

He didn't respond.

"I'm on my way," I answered. This wouldn't be my first crime scene, but it would be my first TNK scene in my current capacity and it would cut my soul.

Chapter Six

Thursday, December 1, 2016 — four-thirty a.m.
Hells Gate, New York
Crime Scene One
Verse One — Mary, Mary, quite contrary
Mary

I entered the taped-off crime scene. I had stepped into dozens of them but never had I had this kind of reaction. This was personal. On the edge of the city where the forgotten roamed was where I found myself on the first of December. I stood three feet from the remains — the newest kill for The Nursery Killer. Squinting through the police lights, I scanned over the large chunks of meat, unsure of what to focus on — shoulders, legs, arms, all of a different shade of red and purple, covered in suet and coagulating blood. I saw the remnants of a torn and jagged breast, placed in one of the hands. It was the only way I could tell if the victim was a male or female.

Her body was splayed out and looked like a morbid mannequin. Her esophagus and arteries were sticking out to resemble rubber tubing. The smell... That smell could only come from recently slaughtered animals. In this case, the animal was human and her body wasn't nearly as warm as freshly butchered livestock. The smell of blood, garbage and released bowels filled my nose. It made me gag. The wind off the river pushed the stench deeper into my lungs and pores. I breathed in trying to calm myself and regretted it the moment I could taste the night on the back of my tongue. I would have given anything to smell something other than death. The odor was the most disturbing thing I had ever breathed in.

The ground surrounding the scene was untouched and white as death, frozen and hellish. It was as though the teeth of winter had bitten off a chunk of Hades and spit it onto the ground around the newest victim. My pulse remained a constant rollercoaster while the questions we all had raced through my mind. *Who did this? Why this victim? Why here? Why now? How the hell do we catch this sick fucker?*

Two eyes looked back at me from the mass of parts and carnage, bulged under the thin blue-tinged lids. I had never given a second thought to the customs of closing someone's eyelids once they had died. But having the vic's dead eyes staring up at me, I wanted to reach out to close them. The lifeless eyes reflected the predawn clouds above. Their dark beauty was lost to the fatality of the night. No matter the cameras or police lights that moved around her, she would never flinch at the flashes or react to the macabre attention paid to her. Her manicured nails, now sprinkled around her, would be her final grasp at life. I couldn't take my eyes off hers. I wanted her to blink, to sit up and patch herself back together.

Her face, which was once probably a thing of beauty, had large chunks of flesh missing. Her cheeks were mostly devoid of skin and meat. The small patches left were hanging in ebony globs, exposing the torn muscle and bone underneath. A painful death was frozen on her face, twisting it into a snarl, her final eternal cry to her God.

Hale passed me a white card wrapped inside a clear evidence bag. I appreciated that he skipped the superfluous small talk and cut to the horror at our feet in Hells Gate.

Mary, Mary, quite contrary.

I read it out loud.

Hale sighed and pulled another bag from his side pocket and handed it over. "Found inside the vic's mouth."

I now knew why he had sent an officer to my house. My stomach rolled.

Hello, Mary,
I was happy to hear you have come out to play.
I have watched you for some time.
I watched you before I painted your walls with dear, sweet Henry.
It was a difficult decision — you or him.
I knew that if I let you live, you would take this adventure to a whole new level.
I will see you soon.
Signed,
The one percent.

P.S. I am not a fan of the nom de plume, The Nursery Killer. Be glad I am not interested in those things, little Mary.

I passed the bag back to Hale and rubbed my temples. "Who all knows I'm helping you with this case?"

Hale shrugged. "A few, mostly cops. I guess your class would have caught on, teachers perhaps?"

"Fuck," I groaned. "Just great."

Hale studied the letter, frowning. "The one percent, as in The Occupy Movement?"

I shook my head. "I doubt it. I think this has more to do with who the killer is, specifically. If I'm here, it's because he or she is a serial killer, a psychopath – or both. It is suspected that one percent of the world's population is a psychopath."

"Jesus," Hale whispered. "Can this get any worse?"

"But careful what you wish for, Hale. The last time I said those words, I was up to my chin in dead bodies. Let's be thankful this isn't a religious zealot," I said and shuddered at my flashes of memory to crop up. "Remember the people who killed in the name of some unknown god in a UFO? Be happy we're not standing in the middle of that."

"What does he mean by '*not being interested in those things*'?" Hale asked, staring back at the letter from the killer.

"If I had to guess, probably killing babies or children, perhaps," I answered. "Whatever the case, the offender hasn't ever addressed a letter to anyone specific, to my knowledge. Either he knows me in some way, through television, classes or in passing. Or, I could know them and not realize it."

"I have someone at your house, searching your yard. Until they search your home, you can't go back there. Even if there is nothing, I'd feel better if you stayed in a hotel until this is over. If this sick bastard is gunning for you, we have you covered," Hale said. He probably noticed my face paling.

"Check my office also," I added.

"Do you know this rhyme?" Hale asked, holding up the signature white card.

I nodded, my eyes still fixed on the vic. "There are three versions, all relatively the same. Four verses. The most common version is, *Mary, Mary, quite contrary, how does your garden grow? With silver bells and cockleshells and pretty maids all in a row.*"

"Do you have any idea why the perp is using nursery rhymes?"

"There could be a million reasons. Perhaps the loss of a child, a parent, a partner, infertility or maybe he worked in a toy store and was driven mad by the constant children's music. We won't know the significance until he either screws up, tells us or we catch him or her," I said. I rubbed the palm of my hand on my chest. The acid was building and my stomach rolled. "If it's all the same, Hale, I'd like to go pack a few things and check into a hotel. I'll compile this scene with the rest of the information and will meet you at noon. I can't stand here any longer."

Hale nodded and motioned for two officers to escort me back to my home. My vehicle was off limits until they gave it a once-over. I was pretty sure the offender wasn't going to cut my brake lines or blow me up. That wasn't the perp's MO. They would want to be up close and personal. They'd want to have me under their nails until I drew my last breath. A car bomb wouldn't have the same appeal.

The city had come to life in between the time I had awoken until the moment I stepped in my front door. I hadn't gotten used to being back in New York. The streets here were punishing. By day, the shoppers swarmed the streets, blue- and white-collar workers owned the streets and the homeless still starved on the corners with the sex-trade workers. In the coolness of the city, people were regarded as no more important than the cracked sidewalks, chipped signs and rotting dumpsters. By night, the streets belonged to gangs and the drug dealers. Unless there was a complaint from those who ran the city, they didn't venture into the dark shadows. The darkness policed itself. No one wanted the heat. I missed Vancouver. I didn't feel so lost there, but I could never go back.

I opened my door and let the swarm of police enter. Something was unsettling about having my home invaded by people I didn't know. A small sliver of anxiety twitched at the corner of my right eye. I hurried up the stairs to my bedroom and closed the door, leaning my back against the hard wood. I breathed in and out, lying to myself. I knew I would have to leave before I could calm completely. I needed to scrub the stench of the night from my pores. I was sure it would take two hours and a bottle of bleach. I could still smell the crime scene on my body.

I pulled my black suitcase from under my bed, already packed. I grabbed a few extra items from my bathroom and closet. I didn't like the idea of being chased out of my home, again by the same person. It angered me, the way I was being controlled by someone I didn't even know. With another deep breath,

I carried my suitcase down my stairs, ignoring the police traipsing through my home and stepped back out into the chilly morning. The frost hit my lungs and cleared my foggy brain. I was driven to the Four Seasons. Usually I wouldn't spend that kind of money on a hotel, but I thought that if I had to leave my home, I was going to grab whatever enjoyment I could get.

"Hello. You've reached the confidential voicemail of April Norris. I'm either out of the office or in class. Please leave a message."

Beep.

"Hi, April, this is Mary. Please give me a call after morning class. I won't be in the office today and need you to bring me a few files. Chat soon."

I left the message and hung up. April had class at eight and never had her phone on during it. No professor would tolerate a ringing phone. Hell, not even I would put up with that.

The double doors that led into the hotel were held open by two gentlemen and were a pristine glass with golden handles. The lobby was elegant in the least classy way possible. It had all the opulent items without the slightest touch of personality. Maybe that was deliberate, in a wealthy-beyond-imagination sort of way. Or perhaps it was because we are attracted to places devoid of such things, removal from the reminders of the chaos of the world we live in. The floor was tiled in black and white marble that echoed every step. It shined as well as any polished glass. There were flowers and trees and arrangements of plants that said they had full-time staff just for that one job. Leaning in to smell, I realized their stamens had been removed to prevent even the pollen from disturbing the marble pedestal tables. The desk, attended by two men and two women, had me checked in within minutes. My room, three hundred square feet, had run almost fifteen hundred a night. It wasn't as flashy as the lobby, but it was still better than pretty much every hotel I'd ever stayed in.

Once the police left me inside the room and I was safe behind the locks, I performed my usual hotel routine. I stopped and sat for ten minutes to ground myself in my surroundings. I closed the curtains, checked all drawers and cabinets then unpacked. Next, I turned on the shower. I pulled off my clothes and dumped them into a laundry bag for room service. I was sure that the smell would surprise them as much as it had me this morning.

I answered my cell phone on the first ring. "Dr. Grant."

"It's Hale. Are you all right?" he asked.

It took me a moment to realize he couldn't see me nodding. "Yeah, I'm good."

"Call me if you need someone to talk to."

"Do you offer all of your colleague's personal therapy sessions or just the ones you're sleeping with?" I asked and regretted it. It was my anxiety talking.

"Everyone left that scene pretty shaken up, including me. Like I've told everyone else who was there, I'm here if you need. If you're not going to call me, call someone, but don't keep it bottled up," Hale replied. He sounded insulted, and I didn't blame him.

"Sorry, Hale. Thanks. I'll call you if I need to." I hung up before I could say something else that was shitty — or worse, invite him to my room.

The crime scene had been brutal. I knew I was being shitty to Hale because it felt like the only thing I could control in the midst of the chaos. I was also still angry over finding out he was FBI. It wasn't even rational anger. I was angry because my lie was over, because I had to face reality once more and because I couldn't go to him and have him hold me as he had. Without him even knowing it, he'd held me while I'd struggled with my pain. He'd never once asked questions when I'd cried silent tears. Even though he'd heard the emotion in my voice, he'd never said a word. Instead, he'd spoken softly to me about nothing, about life, about love, about triumph. It wasn't his fault that it had ended, but I couldn't help but be mad. I took my anger to the shower and prayed I could peel it from my skin.

Rather than standing and scrubbing, I sat in a ball and cried. I needed it. My soul craved the cleansing of a hard sob. The heaviness from Hells Gate was still resting in my limbs and bones and buried in my mind. The stress spread through my body like ink on paper. I took deep, ragged breaths, releasing them into the water and down the drain. Pruned, scrubbed and wrapped in a housecoat, I made a few notes while they were still on the tip of my tongue. I nibbled on breakfast that had a cardboard taste. I scheduled a wake-up call for two hours then let myself sleep. It would be the kind of sleep that mimicked unconsciousness and less of a rested sleep, but I'd take whatever I could grab. With Hale on my mind, I was out cold.

Chapter Seven

Thursday, December 1, 2016
New York
Received and printed by The Wall Street Journal

Letters from a deranged mind,
When the evening lights come on, it gives me the briefest glimpse of each of your faces, like a frozen picture I'd like to burn. I can see your evil smiles twitching at the corners of your chops. You are all skeletal and deranged and soaked in the blood of those you've destroyed. Your eye sockets are filled with inky pools of hate and hysteria, and we share the same disgust for our fellow man. The yellow glow of your fading souls, like the slow death of a lightbulb, only concretes my notion that you all deserve to die. You yank your children up and down the sidewalks as though they're nothing more than fucking pets on a leash. They stare up at you and they, too, wish for your death. Their eyes hold no lies, not like yours. I relish in the knowing I will remove your eyes. Perhaps I should send them to your caged children as gifts.

Insanity is your curse, not mine. I'm cured. I'm absurdly sane. In fact, I bet I'm much safer from the edge of insanity than anyone else. I see life for what it is, not what it could be. Who the fuck lives like that? That is absolute madness. It's right up there with praying for your child to get better but not going to see a doctor then not understanding how you boiled your child to death in their fever. You, Momma and Poppa, are fucking crazy to the nth degree. You are at the top of my list of people I would kill, for no other reason than to rid the world of painful stupidity.

You all fear sanity, having to behave in a reasonable manner. Your once-strange thoughts that sank you into a life you should die for will be removed, leaving you with the truth of the piece of shit you really are. Instead, you walk through life your own little hero – the main character who has overcome obstacles and horror, elevated above all else while forgetting everyone you fucked over to get there. Your delusion of grandeur is just one of the many reasons I will peel your skin like a ripened potato. You are cursed. I would sooner fuck a sewer rat than allow you to breathe another breath. You have not overcome horror. You have no idea what horror is, but I will show you. I will play such fantastic and horrific games with you that fear will develop a new meaning altogether. We will start with your polished fingernails. Tell me… How do you want me to fuck you while I'm pulling the nails from your hands? Don't squirm. I only want to fuck you like you've fucked everyone else. Perhaps, in the ass, as you've done so many times. You know exactly what I'm talking about.

But, I suppose, I do prefer you all that way.

In my nightmares, I am trapped in a rubber room. My mind is clear with no trace of ticks of madness. Being here in New York is a little too close to my own nightmares. You are a personal hell for me. Cheap filth runs the streets, and none of you have the fucking balls to clean it up yourselves. Rest assured. I'm here to help.

I want to help.

Why don't you ever ask me to help you?

Why must you fucking ignore *me?*

I hope you die, either by my hands or the scum in the streets. You would deserve it. You all would. Each of you is guilty of every fucking sin there is. The church can't save you. You'd have more luck at fucking Walmart. You lack the intellectual capacity to understand what I'm saying. Let me dumb this down for the dropouts – the crack heads, the whores living off blow, the moms and dads who are too drunk to feed their kids, the wives too busy sucking another man's cock to pay attention, and the husbands who are deafened by someone else's thighs wrapped around their greedy heads. Each one of you was a wasted chance at abortion. Do me a favor. Save me time and energy with hunting you down. End it now, tonight, yourself. You'd be doing the world a service. Just ask your God. I'm sure he'd agree with me.

Call me crazy, but I am not *the one who is crazy. I am* not. *If you'd like to call me that, I can show you how demented I can be. I will show you. I showed that last bitch, who called me a lunatic to my face, just how nuts I could be. I showed her. I kept her eyes pinned open so she could see. I danced with her while she bled out because that's what crazy does. I killed her, not because she called me a fucking maniac. No, I beat her to a pulp because of that. I killed her because I knew what she liked to do in her free time when she thought no one was watching. One day you'll see. Even if I had been crazy, I did the city a favor. I did your children a favor. You will never realize this and will never be thankful. I killed her for* you!

Mary, Mary, quite contrary... I'm happy you're back to play. We shall see how your garden grows. You shouldn't cry so much, My Mary. You shouldn't drink so much, My Mary.

You should learn to fucking listen, My Mary. Listen for once.
That's what Henry used to say when he drove his fat cock in
and out of every dirty cunt he could find. My Mary, My
Mary, My Mary, My Mary, My Mary, My Mary, My
Mary. You are My Mary.

I hope you liked that display I left for you. I had you in
mind the entire time. You are always on my mind, my
contrary Mary. I left her as my gift, so you would know I
haven't forgotten about you. I was going to kill you. You
know that, right? But I saved you. You're welcome.

Until we meet.
Your friend always, TNK

* * * *

Brock

Another body, another calling card, another letter
and another fucking nightmare for the city. For me, this
was 'just another day in the office'. I had grown used to
always being in the trenches and saying yes to every
file that came across my desk. I didn't question it. No
one makes it very far in the FBI without being a 'yes'
man. The very first sniff of insubordination or
questioning and ten to one your career turned into
something that resembled a tumbleweed. I was pretty
good at nodding at the right time and taking on shit
that would stain the mind, probably all that child
trauma and abuse. As it turns out, there was a silver
lining in there. There wasn't much they could pass my
way that made me flinch. With a sanity nicely callused
in my own personal brand of hell, I closed case after
case. The convictions stuck better than gum on a shoe.

I was born FBI from my toes to my nose. I looked it, breathed it, ate it, slept it and lived it.

I was clean cut, the ladies found me handsome and I was the recipient of a humor bypass. But humor didn't pay the bills, efficiency did. If you wanted things done and done now, I was your man. From the moment I'd known what the FBI was, I'd wanted in. Backing up my hard-earned muscle was my perfect aim, flawless sight, unfailing instinct and faultless paperwork. But I can't keep a girl. I cycle through them faster than razor blades and condoms. The job had always come first, and I couldn't stand the thought of it not being front and center. The first time I'd have to put a girl second, they'd pout, and I'd move on. I couldn't risk them pulling me off track. In that way, my attractiveness was a curse. They allowed me to bail on a woman rather than work it out or improve in any way. But that changed when I had met Mary. I'd started blowing off the overtime just to see her. I'd kept my phone on silent when I'd been around her. Fuck, until her, I hadn't even known how to turn my ringer off.

Seeing Mary work the crime scene had been strangely arousing. Her eyes scanning for the smallest details made me almost reach out to touch her. I found it intoxicating, her brilliance and her ability to shut the door on the world and focus in on the situation that needed her. Mary had every quality I'd ever searched for in a woman. I'd always settled for someone who had one or two of them, but Mary was the full-meal deal. Not only a romantic interest, but she had the skills I had admired in a damn good detective — intellect, courage, discretion and common sense.

The newest letter was like a bullet to the chest. TNK was calling Mary out, taunting her. I knew now that she was the primary target. I had the strongest urge to march over to her hotel, pack her things and place her on a plane to the middle of nowhere with me her sole protector. I could envision myself standing over her sleeping body with a gun and knife, ready and willing to kill anyone who approached her bed. Seeing her name in print, both in the vic's mouth and in the paper, had pulled at my most archaic need to protect her.

"Fuck," I groaned to myself.

I had it bad for Mary and I knew it. How the hell would I be able to focus, knowing I wanted to push her against the wall and shove my cock inside her? I couldn't get it out of my brain. The last time I'd had her, I'd had her against a wall, her legs wrapped around my hips. Every single time she invited me into her pussy, it was better than the last. One touch and that was all it took. It was always that way with Mary. She was the electricity humming under my skin, the reason I lost human instinct and let the animal inside me make all decisions. And although we had agreed to be nothing more to each other than sex, from there on in it was all intense passion. She was intoxicating. She was my release, my escape from the insurmountable horror I faced daily. She was my drug. I had become a force of nature, born to love like a hurricane—to rip out what was rotten so that new growth has a solid footing.

"Fuck," I muttered again. I was falling for her and I was falling fast.

I would see her tomorrow. I wouldn't touch her, but it would take everything I had to be a professional. For the first time in my life, I questioned my abilities around a woman. I had never once doubted myself and I'd always had perfect control. I had the pick of most women in any bar. Good genetics let me be an unbashful whore. I'd slept around, never attaching. It was easier that way. I hadn't bothered lying to myself. This was easier for me and only me. Attachments were something that could be used against you, something that could hurt you and fuck you up six ways from Sunday. No thanks. Been there, done that, and am still paying for my last lawyer.

I palmed my cock, praying for enough of a release to let me sleep. Any other time, I'd have picked up some random woman from a bar and had her suck the release from my body but not this time. I would hate myself for it. I closed my eyes and remembered what it felt like to be inside Mary. Nothing short of electrocution could mimic Mary. I breathed in as deep as I could, my brain almost able to recall her scent. Her hair and skin smelled of vanilla and lavender, but the moment I hit her thighs, it was a scent that hardened my cock. Her taste was exquisite, like nothing I had tasted before. The flavor of her orgasm, to me, was what booze was like to a wino. I needed more.

With each random thought, I brought myself closer then shot my orgasm across my thighs and chest. I clamped my jaw shut to keep myself from screaming Mary's name. It wasn't enough. It wasn't satisfying. It was a drop in the bucket of need. Groaning, I cleaned myself and crawled back into bed, punching my pillow. Nothing would ever be enough unless it were Mary herself. *Love sucks*. The moment I thought the word 'love', I knew I was in a bottomless pit of trouble.

Chapter Eight

Friday, December 2, 2016 – noon
One Police Plaza, New York
Mary

I was tired as hell, weary with a disheveled mind. I could easily pull off the walking zombie look – dead on the inside, yet consciously awake. It was as if my energy was leaking out of me like a draining battery. My exhaustion made me slouch. Every step was a fight against gravity. What I wanted was sleep, real sleep, the kind everyone else has. Hell, I'd take a rough night of it over what was usually dished up for me. I wanted the chaos to leave my mind, leave me in peace to heal.

My sleep, closer to a power nap, was a tussle of conflicting thoughts and nightmares. I wanted to wake up. The longer I stayed in bed, the longer I sat in my subconscious hell. Sixty minutes felt like sixty hours, stuck in a loop of memories I hated. I knew that between now and the day the offender was captured, I would struggle with those memories, not able to get past them. Each time I had jerked awake, I had reached for my phone. I had dialed Hale but had lacked the guts to hit Send. I knew I could have come up with some random reason to call him, just to hear his voice. I'd put my phone down each time and cursed myself for being weak.

One Police Plaza had been built back in God-knows-when out of bricks. The walls were as thick as a castle, and the windows look out at the city with heavy stares. The building reminded me of a prison. The screams from inside were a reminder of one. It was one of the busiest stations I had ever been in. The air hung. It had a weight to it that I could feel on my shoulders when I walked through the front doors. Hale was waiting for me. I had called him while I had been walking up. I didn't like to wait in the front, listening to the sobs and pleading parents of missing children.

When my gaze found Hale, the tension in my shoulders eased up. Hale appeared how I felt—exhausted. His once freshly pressed black suit was wrinkled as though he'd slept in it. The bags under his eyes said the sleep wasn't enough. I caught the small smile that had spread across his face when he had seen me. I wanted to run to him and wrap my arms around him. He had a touch that always chased the nightmares back into the pits where they belonged. Instead, I shook his hand and gave him a professional nod. Once he got a visitor's pass clipped to my white dress shirt, he took the lead and I followed. I liked that he didn't try to make small talk. Once, he might have, but I knew the expression on my face had said not to bother. I wasn't there to get to know him. I was there for The Nursery Killer.

Hale pushed open the doors to a larger office. The walls were covered in crime scene photos, photocopies of the little white cards with nursery rhymes and random pieces of evidence. There was a long black metal table in the center of the room with chairs around it. Boxes of files sat, ready for me to pull out their horrors.

"Dr. Grant." Special Agent Morgan Ridley stood from the table. I hadn't seen him since the day he'd come with Hale to interrupt my life.

I shook his hand. "I'd say it's good to see you, but…"

He smiled a polite and forced smile. Ridley was the kind of man who had been born in a suit, had never been a baby or a child. He was standard issue FBI, straight from the assembly line in Quantico. Everything about him was nondescript. Ridley looked like every bomber there ever had been. If anything, he reminded me of every serial killer I had ever interviewed. He was the guy that never stood out. I was sure he came by it naturally. Unlike Hale, who appeared scruffy in his lack of sleep, Ridley was close shaved and spoke clipped words with a baritone voice. Working with him would likely prove difficult. He didn't strike me as someone who could be a gray thinker—strictly black and white—like most of his colleagues would be.

"Are you ready to get started?"

I set down my bag. "If you all could clear the room for a couple of hours? I'd like to familiarize myself with each case, alone without interruption."

No one argued. The room hushed into complete silence. I needed that silence to step into the mind of a killer. Noises cluttered my thoughts and pulled me off the path in my mind. I started on the left, the first murder. I got up close and personal, holding my voice recorder. Every detail I could see, right down to the tiniest detail, I noted. The second murder, my Henry, made me pause. I knew it would. It was a simple photograph, not of the gore and his death, but of him smiling. The carnage, I could numb myself against. The memory of him smiling punched me in the face.

I clutched my recorder, digging it into the palm of my hand, trying to pull myself out of my pain. I could see my reflection in the glossy pictures on the wall. My ghostly gaze stared back at me. I saw past my own eyes to the face that had once meant the world to me. He was my perfection—perfectly imperfect. It was the happy memories that hurt the worst. They reminded me of what I no longer had and never would have. Part of me prayed that one day I'd be free of these memories, but the other part grieved the thought of losing them.

With sheer will alone, I pushed past Henry and on to the next victim and the next. Each scene was not worse or better. They were all horrific in their own right. The same level of horror could be found in each death. The victim was unrecognizable, almost purposely that way, as though the killer had thought twice about leaving her beauty behind for us all to see. At the end of my trip around the room, I took a seat with four letters from the killer to local newspapers. The first one I hadn't seen until now. It was the very first death. Each letter told me the offender was on the edge of a complete psychological break—if it hadn't happened already. The letters were both intelligent and scattered.

"Possible personality disorder," I added to my recording.

I compiled my list of additions to the new profile. The original profile did not fit the bill. After seeing it all, I felt it was further off than I'd first suspected. It seemed as if Hale had rushed through the profiling phase, likely due to pressure from the top. For myself, assimilating the information was as equally important as where that information led. I absorbed the crime scenes, victim profiles, autopsy reports, police reports and, if any, witness statements. From there, I moved on to the classification stage, integrating all information into a framework which classified the offender as 'organized' or 'disorganized'.

I lifted my recorder. "The offender is organized. The scenes are planned well in advance. Every detail is controlled with no forensic evidence left behind. These are not impulsive kills nor are they opportunistic in nature. There are no known sexual acts with the vics, after death."

I took in the room once again.

"Dr. Grant?" Hale poked his head into the room. His eyes held worry and sadness for me. "You ready?"

I nodded. "Come in. I'm ready."

Hale and Ridley stepped back in. Their presence filled it to the brim. The room, which was twenty by twenty, was more of a shoe box filled with warm air. If I had to choose, I think I'd have stuck with Hale. Ridley seemed as appealing as cleaning my ears with a sharp pencil. Hale struck me as someone who didn't miss much.

"Did you review the scene? Did we miss anything?" Hale asked, taking a seat across from me. He didn't seem insulted by the thought he could have missed something. He was fixed on catching the killer and not who was to blame for missing a tiny detail. That was why I had been brought in, to catch what others didn't.

"I don't think you missed anything, Hale, which is odd." I shook my head and opened my bottle of water. The back of my tongue held the taste of stomach acid.

"Grant, my feelings aren't about to get hurt, if you say I missed something."

"No, what I mean is, it's odd that there has never been a single drop of evidence — no hair, no fibers, no fluids, no fingerprints, no shoe prints, nothing. The only thing you've found is some plant left behind in a tire print. I don't think that was an accident. A perp this careful left that on purpose," I said. "They wanted you in New York."

"Or they wanted us to bring you in." Ridley finally spoke. "Why would they want you involved?"

I shrugged. "I've dedicated years to this killer, learning everything I can about him or her. I am also the wife of a victim. This could be nothing more than a game — or I could be the next victim. He may know me or I may know him, which could be a thrill for the killer. I may talk to him or her daily. I may buy my damn coffee from them. I don't know."

The door tapped and creaked open. "Sir, the latest vic. Here's her report."

An officer passed over a file to Hale and closed the door behind him. Some cops, spending a lifetime on the force, do not see what we had taped to the walls. I didn't blame him when he looked at the pictures and paled, wanting out of our little room of horrors. Hale opened the folder and flicked through the pages. He glanced up at me twice, swallowing hard. I didn't need to have a psych background to know he was nervous.

"What?" I asked after he had glanced at me the third time.

"The latest vic has been ID'd. It's your assistant, April Norris."

His words echoed in my ears. April, my only friend, the one who had braved my anger and reached into my soul to unlock the parts of me that would help me heal. With each visit, she would take a tiny piece of pain out of the door with her.

"Come again?" I asked, clearing my throat. I asked again, even though I had heard him perfectly the first time.

"April Norris," Hale repeated.

I let out a deep breath. I wanted to vomit. I lifted a finger and stood, pacing the room. "I will give you a list of those I am closest to. I'm going to need someone to check on them."

Ridley stood and handed me a pad and pen. "We'll see to it."

Ridley left the room, and Hale kneeled in front of me. "I'm so sorry, Mary."

I nodded and blinked rapidly. Hale reached out and gripped my hand. My first instinct was to pull away from him, but I craved his touch, more now than ever. He stroked my knuckles with his thumb. I could almost feel his emotion seeping into my pores. He lifted my hand to his mouth, placed a small kiss on top and stood.

"I'm sorry to ask this, but is there any reason April would be attacked?" Hale asked, trying to sound sympathetic, but I knew he had a job to do. "Never mind. Clearly you're a target."

"Which means the offender is sure my help will lead to their capture," I said, jotting down a few names of colleagues and friends. I didn't have many, but those I did know would need to be protected until this was over. "Let me know when Mr. and Mrs. Norris arrive. I'd like to be there when they are told."

"Do you want to take some time?" Hale asked.

"No. I can't save April now. She's already dead. But I can try to save the others," I answered and passed the list to Ridley when he walked back in. "We don't have time to mourn. Not yet. She won't be any deader if I wait to grieve. When this is over, I'll let the pain in."

"You sound like every cop I know." Hale gave me an approving nod.

After all the deaths and loss, there was little room for sentimentality. It was easier for cops if they didn't think of victims as people while in the middle of a case. They knew, deep down, that they were or had been someone. But while working the case, examining the pictures, sleep came easier if the victims were numbers, files and faceless victims. And when it got tough, their sense of humor became twisted and macabre. The dead were given nicknames when they were tossed into a mental mass grave. It was the only way to survive without crawling into a bottle or chewing on the end of a gun. There was only so much a mind and soul could take and understand—one new drop and a person might snap. So, they joked, they smiled, they laughed and they coped because they couldn't bring it home. After years of working shoulder to shoulder with cops, I'd learned how to eat a sandwich while looking at a dead body and talking about tap dance lessons and ballet recitals. The first thing I'd learned was that life had ended for them—not for me, not for us.

I would grieve for April but not yet. One day soon, I prayed, I would grieve for all who had suffered. I would allow myself to be ripped open by the blast of my pain. Right now, I would hold it back and let it be the force that pushed me forward.

I retrieved my notes and shifted around the room with Hale and Ridley, pointing at little details I had noticed, like footprints going the wrong way, slight discolorations on the walls indicating missing photos or moved objects. Holding photos at different angles, revealing similarities between scenes. Placing all the photos together and linking the victim's hands, they almost formed a perfect heart. Three more bodies and it would be one.

"What the fuck?" Ridley whispered, surprising both Hale and me. "A heart?"

I nodded and pulled the letters out, along with notes on each victim. "There are usually common traits between victims, but so far, no connections have been found. Some were upper class and some were lower. All had varying ethnic backgrounds, taxonomy, sexes, sexual orientations, religions, some drove and some walked. There were no links. Without the links, the MO could be harder to nail down. At times, the motive wasn't realized until the killer was caught, or if by some fluke, they figured out the motive. It wouldn't help. It rarely does."

"Aside from the heart-shaped death poses, have you found any links or could you hazard a motive?" Ridley asked.

I smiled. "Slow down, rock star. It isn't that simple. I have no clue why the offender is using nursery rhymes."

"The first one, *Ring around the Rosie*... Isn't that about the bubonic plague that struck London in the 1660s? The ring of roses is about the rosy rash, posies were used to ward off the smell of disease and 'ashes,

ashes' are the remnant of cremated bodies. Why would the killer use a nursery rhyme about a plague?" Ridley asked.

"I once thought that's what the rhyme was about too, but it's not," I answered. "*Ring around the Rosie* isn't about the bubonic plague. That's a myth. From what I understand, it's about a religious ban in the nineteenth-century Protestant area in Britain and North America. People found ways around it."

"So, would this signify finding a way around something?" Hale asked.

"Like murder?" Ridley asked and smiled.

"Like a punishment for doing something you're not allowed to do," I answered. "That would be my guess."

"*Three Blind Mice*, the story of Queen Mary the First and her execution of Protestant leaders who were blind to her version of the truth," Hale added and shrugged. "I read it on Facebook."

I laughed. "There are several speculations on the origin and meaning behind that one, but that appears to be the most common meaning."

"The perp killed those who couldn't see the truth?" Ridley asked.

"What were they blind to?" I asked, more to myself than anyone else. I made a note to dig into their lives a little deeper. "*Diddle, Diddle, Dumpling, My Son John...* That one is a nonsense rhyme with no particular historical or political message."

"I remember my dad sang it to me when I was a child," Ridley said. "My grandfather, too."

"I remember hearing it when I was a kid also," Hale added.

I nodded. "Yeah, same here. Maybe that alone is the meaning. It has no importance historically, but there could be a personal meaning to the offender. The death of a parent perhaps…" I trailed off and went back to each picture and file. "Children," I spoke up. "Every single victim had children in their lives in one way or another. They either had their own or were close to a family who had children. They were around children every single day—all of them. That is the only link they have."

"They were killed for having children?" Ridley asked, scrunching his face, confused.

I glanced up and forced myself not to roll my eyes. "Let's consider this from the other side—the offender's. Did they lose a child? Did they want children but can't have them? Were they harmed as a child? Or perhaps they witnessed their siblings abused? Or, do they just fucking hate kids? Are they jealous? Let's look at the vics. How were they involved with children? Any complaints? We need to talk to the kids. There may be more there than we don't know."

"Are you suggesting the killer is taking out people who offend against children?" Hale asked.

I waffled my hand. "I don't know, Hale, but this is as close to an MO as we have. The commonality between all vics is children. Why? Why would that be the only link unless it was important?"

"What about the last rhyme? *Mary, Mary, Quite Contrary*?" Ridley asked.

"'Contrary'… That's one way to describe a murderous psychopath," I answered. "As the story goes, it's a recounting of the homicidal Queen Mary the First, aka Bloody Mary. Silver bells and cockleshells are torture devices."

"Another 'Mary' rhyme," Ridley said, writing down notes.

"My son John…" I trailed off. "Maybe it's the name in the rhyme and not the verse itself. Mary Magdalene is in the Gospel of John. The two were at the foot of the cross. Wasn't Prince John the youngest of the six children born to King George V and his wife, Queen Mary?"

"What about *Ring around the Rosie*? That has nothing to do with any Mary," Ridley said then turned to me. "Never mind. You are the Mary, aren't you?"

I nodded. "We could chase our tails in circles trying to figure out the reasoning behind the nursery rhymes. It could be that they are the offender's favorites. It could be anything."

"Why are you being targeted? Clearly, this is about you," Hale said.

I shrugged. "I don't know. I may have entered the offender's sights in Vancouver. Perhaps I was the original target. The first victim's mother has the first name of Mary. The offender may have lost a child named Mary, a mother, a sister, a wife or friend. This could be a coincidence, but I doubt it."

Ridley stood. "I'll get cars to the addresses you've given me."

"I'll start working on a profile," I said and stood.

"I don't want you alone, Mary," Hale leaned in and whispered.

"You can't watch over me, Hale. You'd never do it for anyone else," I countered.

Hale exhaled a long breath and ran his hand through his hair. "Fine, but you have a two-man detail until this is over."

"For me, this will never end," I whispered. "I will always have this in my life. It's like a scar that no one can see."

"This has scarred us all," he answered, and I walked out.

I didn't know what bothered me most—being a possible target again or not knowing who the offender was after. Crawling inside a psycho's mind wasn't a walk in the park. Figuring out what made them tick added to my reasons why I couldn't sleep at night. This was different from every other case I had worked on. This was personal and becoming more so as each day passed. If I was a target, learning what made their gears turn might be the only thing standing between me being a new victim and TNK being captured.

Chapter Nine

Saturday, December 4, 2016
New York
Received and printed by The New York Times

Letters from a deranged mind,
You still think I'm mad, don't you? I hear you talk about
me with unmoving lips. I hear you whisper my name and
taunt me to come face to face with you because you will give
me a taste of my own medicine. I don't need medicine. I'm
not crazy. Oh, no, I am not crazy, not at all. You are. But I
forgive you and your ignorance. I forgive your reduced
intellect. One can't anticipate society to have any more
brains than those teaching you. I do not expect more from you
than I would the average titmouse.
I will forgive you when I open your eyes wide to the world,
taking your eyelids with me in my fancy tin. I like your eyes
open – wide open. I want you to see how sane I am in my
carving of you. I want you to see how much terror sanity can
bring – much more than the sick mind could ever create for
you. No. You need sanity to create artwork like mine.

I will forgive you and your words as I slowly slice the tongue from your gaping, lie-filled mouth. You will never tell another lie, not when I have your tongue in my pocket. Why must you fucking lie? But I'm not the type to hold a grudge. I will forgive the lies. But, I will not allow you to make the same mistake twice, so I shall keep your lying little tongue with me, tucked deep in my pants, licking at my asshole where it belongs.

Humanity is a slow-moving train wreck with bodies and limbs being spat out from under the bloody wheels. Most of you notice the trail of blood and gore. Many of you choose to ignore it, even when you're hit with limbs and guts. You're oblivious in your ignorance. Watch what I do when you ignore me. You can't be ignorant to your intestines wrapped around your neck in a pretty bow tie. But it will be too late — always too late.

When I asked about the love you have for your family, you tell stories of happiness, but leave out the prison cell that makes up the walls of your home. But you didn't just build a prison, did you? No, you poured pure loathing and hate into its design. It's nothing more than a glorified pine box waiting for a soul to fill it. Which baby will you kill? Which one will you rest a pillow on top of and claim they died in their sleep? It's not really how you thought it would be, is it? Children aren't like whores. You can't just wring their necks when you've had your fill.

If I am disgusted with you, I know you feel it, too. What disgusts you about you? What do you do that makes your skin crawl? What is repellent about yourself? Then ask yourself, do you enjoy it? Does it make your cunt wet and cock hard? Why? For once, be fucking honest. I guarantee you won't like the answer. I promise you will find the reason I am hunting you inside you. I have seen what you have done. I saw it all. Not a single detail missed my eye. And you know you will be caught, eventually, but just one more time was needed, then you'd stop. Isn't that right? But did you stop? No. You will never *stop. You could have, you could have killed yourself for me. Yet, you did not. The sight of you makes me sick from my toenails to my ears. Hate for me isn't something that happens overnight, but I know evil when I see it, and my hate for you was instant.*

Do not call me sick. I am not *sick. I am good. I am sane. I am in control. I control you. You are mine to do with as I please. Stop looking at me like I'm crazy. I* hate *you. You fucking disgust me. I need you to die. I need to watch it. I want to be touching your heart when it stops. I will feel better once I do that. I will be better. I am doing this for everyone else. You are welcome!*

Take it from me, brain sickness – being crazy, insane – sounds amusing, not so much from the inside. Imagine your worst nightmare. Think of it. Bring it forward. Now imagine that you can't wake up from it because you are already awake. I know you want to know if that's what happened to me. I don't want to talk about what made me snap. Don't be offended. I don't know you very well, yet. I'm sure I'll tell you all about it while I'm cutting off your ears. Maybe that's what worries you? Oh, I get it. You think what I have is contagious. I wish it were. I wish everyone felt the need to toss out the trash. Well, I won't lie to you. There are perks to snapping. I don't recommend it, not for anyone and least of all you. You are too weak for this life. You're adorable in your frailness, flailing around, trying to keep your head above water. I wish I were the one standing on your head. I'd let you breathe, for a moment.

I liked seeing your face, Mary. You shouldn't cry so much. Your eyes are too puffy to be beautiful now. How do you expect a new man to fuck your starved cunt when you look like shit all the time? That is why your Henry liked you on your hands and knees, facing away from him, so he didn't have to see your face. One would think you'd be happy not to have to deal with his shit day in and day out. Maybe now you can have a baby and be happy. But you need to open your legs, Mary. I can help you. Why didn't you just mind your own business? Why did you have to get involved? Why are you here, Mary? Now I have to kill you, too. Is that what you want? Am I your suicide? Why, Mary? Why?

Until we meet.

Your friend always, TNK

* * * *

Brock

I spent hours reading up on nursery rhymes, flicking back and forth between old fables and truer-than-life origins of little songs we sing to children before they sleep. I wondered how songs about beheading and torture could turn into something we taught to children in cheerful glee. My stomach turned at the history of man. In comparison, it didn't feel like we had made much progress. People still killed with the same amount of ease and satisfaction, only now it was more expensive to prove it. In the list of great horror writing, Mother Goose wasn't all that far behind. She had a dark streak that most writers couldn't touch. The disturbing theories and stories behind some of the most favored rhymes left me speechless.

Reading the newest letter from TNK, I had morphed from a need to catch him to save the public into a personal hunt for me. Every word written had felt like a stab to my chest. Reading her name in the paper sent my balls into my stomach and boiled my blood. The growing need to bring down TNK before TNK caught Mary drove me to near insanity. I hadn't needed to focus this much attention to my temper. Now, I was on the edge of snapping at the next person to ask a stupid question. I knew I should speak to my direct supervisor about my existing relationship with Mary, but I didn't want to risk not being here to protect her. I supposed I didn't have a relationship with her, not to her anyhow. To me, the sex was great, but I wanted more of her, all of her, including a heart that had been smashed against the rocks and taken for a joyride by the same sick fuck who was toying with her now. I should have felt some sort of shame, wanting her broken heart to be mine.

We were all sitting and waiting for something to happen and praying we'd have a lead, something to help us shut this shit down for good. And while we were waiting, I was dreading it. I feared the next moments. I didn't want to come face to face with TNK. I feared Mary would be next, even with my eye on her. I was scared the capture of TNK would come in the form of me finding TNK strung up in Mary's own web of flesh. Realistically, TNK could have taken her as the first victim. Right now, anyone was a potential vic, and I felt like shit for praying it would be anyone other than her. I couldn't wait for this to be over, to have a chance with Mary. She was the one who could keep me in line, keep me on the straight and narrow and help me patch up what was still dangling from my heart.

I rotated my cell phone in my hand, debating on whether or not to punch in her number. I had dozens of reasons to call her. We were working the same case and she was being targeted by a serial killer. But I had more reasons than I could count to leave her alone. The wound she was standing in, the reminder of a tragedy that had taken everything from her, was enough for me to put my phone down and scold myself. *How can I move on when I can't breathe without her? How do I let her go when it feels like she is the only thing keeping my head above water?*

"I'm fucked," I mumbled to myself.

Isn't love supposed to be less painful and tormenting? I guess that was why love was invisible, to a degree. I saw love all the time. I saw it in the way people smiled, lifted vehicles off their children, jumped in front of bullets and laughed to themselves. Aside from our actions, it was virtually undetectable with anything but our minds. We probably weren't evolved enough to be trusted with something like love. We'd screw with it. It was in our nature to try to manipulate something, weaponize it. If someone were to have given love to me in the form of a fragile glass heart, I'm sure I would have smashed it on the ground. Life seemed much easier when you weren't always worrying about someone else — or that was the lie I was going to stick with. It was easier than admitting I'd be so fucking lost without her.

I lost my fight with my own brain. My heart pulled a haymaker, and I picked up my phone and dialed Mary.

"Hey, Hale," she answered. "Please don't fucking tell me we have another one."

"No, no, I'm just calling to see how you're doing," I answered. "I didn't wake you, did I?"

"I'm awake, like everyone else. I'm doing okay. How about you?" Mary asked.

"I'm worried for you. I know, I know…not all that professional, but, I'm still worried. Do me a favor, please? Don't go anywhere without letting me know or having me there?" I asked, praying she wouldn't make a big deal out of it.

She sighed. "All right, I'll keep you apprised of when I leave and where I'm going. And, Hale, thanks for worrying. As irritating as it normally would be for me, I appreciate it."

"You're welcome. Goodnight, Mary."

"Wait. Hale? Can we talk for a bit longer?" she asked.

A lifeline. I'd take it. I didn't want to hang up. "Of course. What about?"

"Anything, nothing, just something to take my mind out of the darkness. Since you know pretty much everything about me, tell me about you."

"Get comfortable. It's a long story." I rolled onto my back. I eased into the horror with a few bits about my career and training, friends, my new life in New York and about the moment I'd first seen her. I poured out my heart and held nothing back.

"I had no bladder control when I was younger and no one ever wondered why. A wet bed meant a beating with whatever was lying around—a shoe, a book and once a lamp. I remember my mom had started asking if I wanted a 'slippering'. She'd take off her plastic-bottomed slipper and would slap me with it. She'd out me in front of the other kids. Along with the slipper came mocking and teasing. It even happened at school. I'd be sitting there happy as a clam then the home bell would sound and I'd piss my pants. Not a single teacher would stop me to ask why I had wet myself. Hell, no one ever asked why I had black eyes or stunk like I hadn't bathed in weeks. Funny thing, the moment I was removed from home was when I finally mastered the bladder issue."

For the first time in my life, I told the absolute truth, every gory detail. I hadn't talked about my mother like that—the love I still had and the heartache I carried. "Even though I'm not that same kid and life was never easy growing up, I'm thankful for her. The suffering made me who I am today, and in some ways, because I know the depths of hell, my life is better because of it. One day, if I'm blessed, I'll be a father and I pray I do better. I made a vow when I was old enough to understand how brutal my life had been that I'd be everything my mother wasn't and give my children all of my heart and soul."

I told her about every home I had been in, some worse than my mother's and some better. I hadn't told anyone the truths I was now telling Mary. I hadn't realized how much of my life I had held back from those I had thought I loved. It was almost cathartic to hear my pain out loud. I had felt no shame opening myself up like a carnival of raw emotion. In return, she told me about her upbringing and the wounds that were not yet healed.

"Out of all the moments I'd rather forget, I will never forget dinner." Mary sighed. It was as if I were witnessing the taking off of a long, scabbed-over Band-Aid. "There was always so much tension in the house. My father teetered on the edge of his rage, like at any moment he would blow and clear the table with his fists. My mother, in her drunken, sullen withdrawal from the world, was always two steps away from zeroing in on me with a critical speech of my adolescent failures. Keep in mind, nothing short of perfection would be tolerated in my household. Being a child, perfection was out of reach. I still remembered constructing volcanoes from mashed potatoes. I did what I could to keep my eyes on my plate and not test my fate by making eye contact with either of them."

Mary sighed. "The trick—probably something you can relate to—was to do everything right, be perfect, smile, nod and keep your mouth shut, otherwise the rage they weren't showing each other would find a new and smaller target."

Mary's voice had changed halfway through her story. There was an angry bite to it. Her resentment died when she spoke about her parents' deaths. She and I had more in common than I had thought. Our memories, good and bad, had woven the fabric of who we now were. Story after story, we shared our rawness. It had felt like minutes had passed, but when I looked at the clock, hours had eaten away. Mary's yawn had triggered my own.

"Thank you, Hale," she whispered, her voice tired and in need of asleep.

"Goodnight, Mary," I replied, and we both hung up.

I felt my grip on my sanity tighten a little more after hearing her voice and her story. Fucking love and the pool of pathetic it had turned me into... My drive to protect her hadn't lessened. If anything, it had increased. I'd chalk it up to some sort of biological protective need rather than admitting I was ten steps away from parking my ass in front of her door with a gun and a knife. The very thought that she was alone in her room made me feel sick to my stomach. I sent a text to the team lead on duty for the night and asked for them to up their rounds on Mary's floor. It was all I could do for now.

Chapter Ten

Wednesday, December 7, 2016 — eleven p.m.
Brooklyn Bridge, East River, New York
Crime Scene Two
Verse Two — How does your garden grow?
Mary

I couldn't shake the feeling that something wasn't right. Everything, from the moment I had woken, was just off. It was like waking in some 1950s murder-mystery show. But it wasn't just that. The weather was very cloudy, colder than usual, with a nip to the wind that slapped my face. No one spoke or smiled at each other on the sidewalks, but today, more than any other time, people looked depressed, scowling, like they had a new chip on their shoulder. I had known it was going to be a bad day and when Hale had called me, I'd known it had become ruthless.

Day had given up its fight for the sky, rolling over for the night. The battle between the two marked the sky with shades of red, orange and pink. It was almost beautiful, the battle. Now, the only thing left behind was a black canvas and a brilliant moon. The darkness was thick and felt smothering. The air was too cold to breathe comfortably. My lungs froze with each breath. Whatever the sun had managed to defrost during the day, the night took hold of and froze once again under its chilled touch. Through the winter, the only problem at night was the blackness. Everything was lost in the dark. The nights were as ferocious as a dip in a frozen river would be.

Other than the darkness, all that seemed to exist was the wind. Its severe bite could be felt through every layer of clothing a person tried to wear. The hairs on my arms raised with the wind, leaving behind a coating of fresh gooseflesh. My blood ran cold, and my marrow slushed to ice. I knew it had less to do with the weather than I gave credit.

Ten feet in front of me stood two tall trees. They glittered under the lights from their fresh coating of frost. Their denuded forms stood starkly against the snow, like charcoal drawings placed on top of the ground. The limbs, once vibrant with life, once unblemished in a white layer, now held death. I could smell the river mixed in. I hated it.

A spiderweb, nearly eight feet in diameter, was strung between the trees and limbs. From thirty feet away, it was beautiful. It was an intricate design, a delicate sculpture of silky thread with added jewels of small droplets of frozen water. It was a thing of such beauty until you could almost touch it. The closer you got, the more horrific it became. The silky thread was intestines. The massive spider in the middle of the web was a male human head, fingers making the spider's legs. The skinned ribcage was used as a planter box, filled with limbs for stems with flesh twisted into flowers, resting on top. Rotting flowers were scattered under the human web.

"How does your garden grow?" I whispered, breaking up the surrounding silence. The scene held the kind of silence that falls right before you get knifed in the back. It was one of those moments that everyone would spend hours trying to wash off in vain.

Taking in the offender's newest artwork, I flinched. I approached the masterpiece. There was a vague sense of familiarity that washed over me the more I inched toward the victim. It took a millisecond for my brain to register the eyes. In life, his eyes had reminded me of a clear, sunny day with a touch of clouds, almost white-blue. His eyes were wide open, fixed from the weather and frozen in fear. I felt a pang of guilt. I knew him, but there was nothing I could have done to save him. So I stared back at his dead, machine-like eyes and felt nothing.

"Do you know him?" Hale asked, stepping up to my side.

I nodded. "Yes and no. He showed up at my hotel a few times when I was traveling. I put a restraining order against him. Last I heard, he'd moved on to someone else and had ended up in jail."

Hale pulled out his little black notebook. "Andrew Walden, age twenty-seven. The last check-in with his PO put him alive at dinnertime yesterday. Arrested for a break and enter, assault with a deadly weapon and attempted child rape."

I almost smiled. The vic had been strung up for harming children. It was no loss to me, not even professionally. I could never condone or even understand harm to children. I knew I couldn't be one of those doctors who helped rapists or child molesters. *Nope. Lock them up and throw away the key.* No amount of education would change my mind on that one. In my heart and soul, I didn't think I could treat the monster out of people like that.

"Don't worry about hiding the smile, Doc. Everyone here is on board with you," Hale said and turned his back on the victim. "We'll bag him and tag him."

I looked away from the human spiderweb. "We may think he deserved this, but we still need every scrap of evidence we can find."

"Like I said, we'll bag it and take it." Hale said, motioning for the gore team to take over and shovel up the mess that that once had been a monster in human form. Hale walked me to his car. They still didn't trust me to drive a vehicle of my own. "Drink?"

I nodded. "I could do that."

The return to the hotel wasn't padded with idle chitchat, useless words people used to fill the awkward silence. We bounced interpretations and notes about the crime between us, like kids kicking a rubber ball. Hale was quick with his questions. Brainstorming was his strength. A person didn't climb the ladder in his career without doing the grunt work. By the time we hit the hotel, we weren't any closer to catching the offender, but we were both on the same page and heading in the same direction. He didn't care how we caught him or who got the credit, as long as they were off the bloody circuit.

Two drinks in and Hale let down his guard and the man I remember peered out. It was a relief, given that I was a walking, talking basket case, barely holding on some days. Until our late-night phone call, he and I had never talked about our real lives, jobs or anything personal. We were there for only one reason. Now, it felt real. He felt real.

"Why do you do what you do?" I asked him.

"There should be a way to stop these things from happening. When someone chooses to wipe out another bunch of human beings, someone should be there saying 'no, no more', someone needs to be there to hold humanity accountable. Why do you do what *you* do?"

I sighed. "Originally, I wanted to help those trapped inside the prisons of their minds, be a refuge for those forgotten by the wider world. For those who are long past help, they're taken in and put in an asylum, which is nothing more than a place for people that no one knows what to do with. It's just a different kind of prison, where you leave your dignity at the door along with your clothes and are medicated into compliance and passive behavior then released back into the world without gaining the help needed."

"And now?"

I drank back my drink, the ice nudging my lips. I raised my glass to signal for another. "Now I want to catch the sick fuck that did this to me. I wish I could say it's for the greater good, for humanity, but he destroyed my fucking life. I need him to be locked away so that I can finally move on."

The bartender placed my drink in front of me, and I lifted it to meet Hale's glass.

He toasted, "To the capture of said sick fuck." Then Hale spoke about his tormented past, and how it had driven him to join the FBI. He wanted to be one of the good guys, someone who rescued those who had lost hope. Life had no color for Hale, no shades of gray, either. He was all black and all white, right and wrong, legal and illegal. Bending the rules wasn't a card in his deck. When he wasn't doing his paperwork — on time, every time — he was combing the streets and taking down perps. That was how he had been from day one. It was the reason he had two marriages under his belt. I was pretty sure he clocked more hours than any of the rest of his team. That was also the reason he and I had met. We'd both dug ourselves into a lonely hole.

I wasn't sure if we got wittier from sleep deprivation when the morning rolled in or if it was just the effect of the liquor. We'd needed the morose venting we'd done. In this job — or any frontline job — a person did what they had to do to get the load of shit off their back. Cruel as it sounded, once the life faded from a victim, there was just another crime to solve and a body to bury. The soul had moved on and the living were tasked with what was left. We all prayed for the dead, but our energy was spent on the living. Part of that energy was finding the SOB, and the other part was figuring out how to stay sane staring into dead eyes when your phone goes off at three in the morning.

The only time a corpse was not a corpse was when someone who loved them entered the room. That was when trauma arrived. Unless that was the case, the deceased was usually dealt with in a macabre humor sort of way. It wasn't that people didn't care. That was why they kept coming back. That was why they worked until they were forced to retire.

"We'll get the guy," Hale said, sounding sure of himself. "I won't stop until we have him in custody, behind bars, rotting."

"It'll never be enough. Not even his death will be payment for what he's done," I answered. It was true. I could wrap my hands around his neck and take his last heartbeat from him, but it wouldn't give me back what I had lost—my future, my love, my life.

Hale ordered two more rounds with a shooter in between. I didn't need it, but it still quenched my tired sanity with the liquid equivalent of pain medication. I had spent plenty of nights inside the bottle, refusing to crawl out. Tonight, I would numb my pain. This time, unlike every other time, I had a friend to clink my glass against, rather than off the floor like I had before. Once, I had been determined to stay drunk until I died. But when death didn't come, I had been faced with the reality of life. Seeing it through booze-soaked goggles was scarier than attempting life while sober.

Hale paid the tab and walked me to my room. I was more than a bit tipsy. I was at the stage of schoolgirl giggling but still far from plateauing into depressive hate. It was the kind of laughter that robbed my lungs. All the anguish and stress of the past few weeks had melted away like ice cubes on a hot stove. It was a small vacation, a blessed relief from all the insanity that had shoved its way into my brain. For a brief moment nothing else mattered. The tightness in my chest, the cramping muscles... They all went away. And with that came hope.

"Thank you," Hale said, pausing in front of my hotel door. "Thank you for not shutting me out."

Two officers sat close by, each one reading a book. I knew there were more in the hotel. I had seen three in the bar, two in the lobby and one in the elevator coming up. Part of me disliked the idea of pulling good cops off the street to be on my babysitting duty. The rationale part of my brain was scared and thankful.

I smiled. For once, I felt relaxed, not on edge. "Thank you. I'll see you tomorrow."

Hale leaned forward. He froze for a moment and stepped back from me. His cheeks were flushed red. "I apologize. I'm sorry. I… I thought maybe… I know we agreed to wait until this is over. I'm sorry."

"Don't worry about it, Hale. We've both had a lot to drink. What seems like a good idea right now probably isn't," I answered. "Are you driving?"

He shook his head. "No. I'm in the room below yours."

I felt instant relief knowing Hale would be a floor away. "Goodnight, Hale." I pulled out my keycard and opened my door. The thought of inviting him into my room had crossed my mind several times on the way up, but I knew I'd hate myself and him in the morning. I had been there, done that. I didn't need another reason to cry or question myself. Hale was a pretty good guy, a great catch, but I needed to put this part of my life to rest before beginning a new chapter.

"Goodnight, Mary," he whispered, leaning into my doorframe. "I miss you."

I turned with a smile and gave him the truth he needed…that we both needed. "I miss you, too, more than you know."

"Soon?" he asked.

I smiled. "Let me put this behind me. And when it's over, I'll find you. I promise."

I closed the door, shutting him out in the hall where I knew he belonged, for tonight at least. Drunk or sober, I followed my night routine and crawled into bed. I was almost asleep before my head even hit the pillow. If I dreamed, I don't remember it. It was one of the perks of borderline alcohol poisoning. I recall hearing him enter the room below me and smiling because I knew my bed was over his. In some small way, we were together tonight.

Chapter Eleven

Thursday, December 8, 2016 – three p.m.
One Police Plaza, New York
Mary

All of April's life she had feared death. It had been her darkest fear, so deep that she'd suppressed dealing with the idea it could happen at any moment. She had never been ready to depart. April had gone through life believing there would be tomorrow and a day after that. But, like all fears, we face them, ready or not. Life and time were no longer her casual acquaintance but had taken her by the throat and dragged her forward and beyond. Death had come for April like a shotgun blast, startling, but not nearly slower than I wished it would have been for her. One moment April had been doing April things, the next she had been going and gone. Given that we all have to die somehow, it had been a less than gracious end for someone I'd once known.

Death was a shadow that lurked in the dark. It slinked around and crawled under people's beds, and it was always there, waiting to strike. For April, death hadn't hunted her slowly. It had come in the form of a psychopath—picking and choosing, forcing the death's hand.

Not until my life had brought me to my knees in front of Henry—and now sitting beside April's distraught parents—did I truly begin to chip away at the thoughts of these messengers of death. April's life had reached its end and my sanity felt thin and as tearable, as paper. Carol Norris, April's mother, struggled to hold in her grief. Her once perfectly applied makeup now ran down her face with the steady stream of tears. I felt bruised inside, a numbness that carried a screeching piece of sadness.

The family room we had been shuffled into was designed to be calming, with light blues and greens. Two long mint-colored sofas were placed in the middle, facing each other. Fake plants and crappy artwork filled the rest of the room, because the grief itself wouldn't fill the room as it was. It was irritating. I wanted darkness, hushed lights and curtains— something that said this moment was life altering, not a palate of cheer splashed on the wall. April would not have liked these colors. She'd always dressed in black with a hint of color, usually crimson red.

Carol had dressed like her daughter. Something about her said she was always ready to appear at a funeral, black from toe to nose, with deep lines that hadn't developed overnight. Carol's sobs would be heard down the hall and into the streets. It was more than crying. It was the kind of wild sobbing that comes from a person drained of everything worth living for.

Karl had barely spoken while he held his wife together, but his pain could be touched in the air. The agony that flowed from him was as palpable as the bitter fall wind. Every now and again he'd stare up at the ceiling, toward heaven. I knew that expression. I had done it after Henry had been taken from me.

Sitting with Carol and April's father Karl, I said goodbye to April. Although her soul was long gone, I pleaded with the man upstairs for one more cup of coffee with her, one more embrace or one more heated debate. I sat in my selfishness, holding on to Carol's hand. I didn't want to be there, but some sort of death etiquette demanded I visited April's parents, offer my condolences and share the best memories I had of her. Somehow, this was supposed to help them while they drowned in grief. I had always kept an appropriate and professional distance with April, but deep down, I had grown to care for her as a friend. She had been there when others had run, and she had picked me up out of my drunken stupor more times that I remember being drunk. Now, all the stories I had of her seemed redundant. She was gone and the rest of us remained. Grief tore at my insides.

Carol let go of my hand and pulled a tissue from her black patent-leather purse. April had had one exactly like it. Carol dried her eyes, and the hurt was replaced with anger. She had cried until there was nothing left inside but anger so deep it nibbled at a person's insides like a hungry rat. Her irises were threaded scarlet and her eyeballs hung heavy in their sockets. The little lines at the edge of each eye deepened.

"You did this. You did this to my April. I told her to come home. I said you would get her killed," Carol snapped at me. She stood and towered over me. "It's because of you. This madman wanted you and took my April instead."

Hale stood from the couch across from us and I shook my head. They needed someone to be angry at, a target, and I was willing to be that person. The fact that they blamed me wouldn't make me lose sleep tonight, though. I knew it wasn't my fault. I cannot control the actions of others. Loss was the other side of love that no one spoke about. I'd take it all from them, every drop of hate, if it meant they could bury April and heal. Carol's pain and temper was a wild storm to be endured, out of respect for April.

Carol screamed and stomped her petite feet. She waggled her finger in my face, and her spittle left a coating on my skin. The burn of the punch left me surprised. Nausea swirled unrestrained in my empty stomach. Hale jumped and pulled Carol back before she could dive for me. My head swam with half-formed thoughts. My heart felt as if my blood had become sludge while it struggled to keep a steady beat. My already melancholy mood took a nose dive and strangled me as though I were gagging on black tar. Karl and Hale dragged Carol from the room, kicking and screaming. She may have been small, but she appeared bigger than a prize fighter.

Hale returned with a blue ice pack. "Are you all right?"

I nodded. "Well, that went better than I thought. April had said her mother had one hell of an Irish temper. I now know what an Irish temper looks like."

Hale pressed the ice pack onto the throb beginning on my jaw bone. His touch sent shivers down my spine. I yanked my mind out of the naked gutter and refocused. This wasn't the first time I had been hit, thanks to my childhood, but it hurt like I had no idea what to expect. This was probably the worst part of any murder. The dead were already dead, and I couldn't do anything about it. Talking to those left behind was pure hell. Their pain was rich enough for it to be felt on the back of my brain like fingernails.

The door opened once more and Special Agent Cole Nelson stepped into the room. His face was grim. He had been in training in New York, or as he called it 'desk duty'. I never asked why he felt that way or what prompted his rear in a desk. He hadn't elaborated and I didn't bother poking at it.

"Sir, I have a package here for you," Nelson said and handed over a small yellow envelope. "It was delivered along with flowers for the grieving."

Hale glanced at me. Frowning, he opened the small envelope. "Did you order flowers for the Norris family?"

I shook my head.

Hale pulled out a white card. His face said it all. He glanced back to Nelson. "Who dropped this off?"

"Flower delivery guy. I have the order form with the flowers. What's up?"

Hale opened the card and read out loud. "Good day, Agent Hall. I am writing this to you for a very special reason. The three-year anniversary for Henry is today. You may not have remembered this. Did it slip your cluttered mind? Perhaps you could have asked her this the last time you were fucking her. Wouldn't that have made the little bitch squirm? It's not like it would have opened up old wounds. Trust me. Those fuckers are still wide open. Is she insulted that you want to drive your cock into her throat but can't remember the simplest details of say…when her fucking husband was killed? Poor manners for a potential suitor, wouldn't you agree?"

I stood, my breath caught in my throat. Today was December eighth. I had tried to ignore the day, pushed it into the back of my mind for later. I had planned on remembering him in my own way, not having it shoved into my face like this.

"Do you want me to stop?" Hale asked, and I shook my head.

He went on, "If you feel uncomfortable dealing so openly with the anniversary, you might simply buy a box of chocolates or some flowers. I've taken care of the flowers for you. Sunflowers. Sure, it's a three-year wedding gift, but what does one buy a gal whose husband was slaughtered? Whatever you decide to do, the anniversary of someone's death is an opportunity to show love and caring, an act of friendship never to be forgotten. You're welcome."

The world swam. The tension I had resting in my shoulders had made its way up into my head and pounded with each word Hale spoke.

"Mary, this is for you," Hale said and passed me a small white card.

I didn't want to read whatever the bastard had written to me.

"It says 'Happy Anniversary' and gives an address," Hale said.

"Another crime scene?" I asked and frowned. "Out of character... It's broad daylight."

Hale stepped away from me and handed the cards to Nelson. He ordered a team to the address and shut the door, giving us privacy. "I'm torn, Mary. I want to hold you and tell you it's going to be all right, but I've got to go. Are you in or out? I need to know."

I tucked the anxiety down and stood. "I'm in."

Chapter Twelve

Mary

The tall, gray and dilapidated building stood in the middle of the empty, abandoned street. The old building would have been a tear-down in any other area of the city, but there's no money in the parts of town that people are afraid to venture into. You can sense the emptiness in the air, like the world had stopped caring long ago about the souls who came there to die. The building appeared as though it had grown there rather than been built. The spray-painted stone made my skin crawl. Warnings in brilliant red told me everything I needed to know. *Turn back*. But we didn't. I glanced up at the rows of newspapered windows and cringed.

I followed in the front door, behind Hale, leaving the gloomy day behind. The threat of a snowstorm became more appealing than stepping into a building that not even the locals would enter. The old wood floors, scuffed from years of footfalls, creaked under our feet. There was nothing right about the building. Something was off. Something scratched the back of my brain and caused me to pause. The chipped paint and décor pulled me into a different era, yanked back twenty years ago when the building had been bustling with business.

The air outside had frozen my lungs, but inside, the air was more like summer than winter, and it was brighter than I would have thought. The air smelled like it hadn't moved in years, festering like a stagnant pool of water. I shined my light ahead, the only movement being the dust our boots had dislodged. Once, years before, they had made dolls here and packaged them for buyers overseas. Little glass eyeballs still sat on the floor. Tiny arms and legs scattered the shelves.

"What happened here? It's like they decided to shut down overnight," I asked no one in particular.

"This used to be an asylum until the government closed the doors for the cruel and unusual treatment of patients. The building was bought by some crazed tycoon. The locals say that one day the owner lost his mind and gutted a girl with a stuffing hook. He was found with the body, the city's first case of necrophilia. It was locked up right after and has been abandoned ever since," the officer behind me answered. "Everyone thinks the place is haunted."

I pointed my flashlight at the floor — paint drips, red. I stared at them longer than I should have, forcing those at the back to wait for me.

"Blood," I whispered, grabbing Hale's attention. He turned with a nod and motioned ahead of him.

A banner hung from the ceiling.

'Happy Anniversary' was painted in red.

Under the banner, a long, banquet-sized table sat, the small candles still burning. Sunflowers had been placed in front of each of the twelve chairs that surrounded the table. One little white box sat in the middle of the table, wrapped in a red ribbon. Two cops opened the box and paused. The world slowed around me. I could hear my pulse in my ears, long and deep vibrations. I watched Hale approach the table after the first two officers turned with pale expressions. Hale leaned over the table then faced me, shaking his head.

"What is it?" I asked.

"You don't need to see this, Mary," he replied.

Never in the history of ever has wording like that caused a person not to look. If anything, it is an enticement. One foot in front of the other, I stood at the edge of the table. I peered into the box. I was slapped with a nightmare without even having to be asleep. The room filled with a strangled scream and faint voices. It took me a moment to realize the screams were from me.

Delicately placed inside the box, sitting on top of red tissue paper, was a finger. A wedding band sat on the end of the finger, just above the torn meat and bone. The wedding band had belonged to Henry. It was an identical match to the wedding band I still wore around my neck on a chain. Seeing his finger had pulled my mind roaring back to me scrambling on the floor of our home, slipping in his blood. I covered my mouth and closed my eyes. I forced myself to count to ten, letting the emotion move through me and out of me with each breath.

"Grant?" Hale called out to me.

I opened my eyes and nodded. "I'm good."

"This was a mistake," he mumbled and grabbed at my arm to yank me from the table.

I stepped away from him. "No, you're not taking me off this now, not after everything I've been through."

He pointed to the door. "Outside... You're too close to this one, Grant. I'm not cutting you out, but you sure as shit are not going to watch us collect the evidence this time."

I glared but walked toward the door. Hale was right. I was too close to it. The evidence was a part of me — my life, my heartache, my Henry. My shoulders hunched when I shuffled down the stairs to the front door. I leaned against the wall that had seen better days, now crumbling under the strain of twenty years ignored. My gaze roamed the graffiti and I found myself nodding. I had been warned about entering these halls, and I'd paid for my ignorance. I dug my nails into the cracks and pits in the stone and knew my sanity was much like this empty building.

The muscle twitched involuntarily at the corner of my right eye, jerking from the stress of sleep deprivation and emotion. I had a rigid grimace, angry at the day. With arms folded now, I tapped my foot while waiting on Hale. Outside, the once-ignored street was busy with badges and uniforms. The dreary day would either see me to dawn or snap me in two.

"Grant," Hale called out, and I spun to face the top of the stairs. He held the corner of a white page, lowering it into a clear evidence bag. "We have something."

Before I could head up the stairs, he was coming down, two at a time. He handed over the bag, inside, a typewritten letter.

Profile of a deranged mind.
My gift to you, Mary Mary quite contrary, is my profile.

I scanned down the typed vignette. It looked like every other one I have read, carefully worded and to the point.

Victimology — Adult offenders, between the ages of twenty-five and sixty, no preference to sex or ethnicities, preference for cheaters, liars, child abusers, victims from all socioeconomic backgrounds

Past Criminal Behavior — prior criminal record unassociated with this crime

Precipitating Events — Explained urges to kill, primarily due to society allowing monsters to walk freely

Offender Demographic — Older white female, thirty-five to forty-five years old, no outstanding physical features, small in stature, harmless appearance, soft-spoken, highly educated in early years, no significant relationships, no close family ties, no interpersonal relationships, no community ties, unremarkable and does not stand out in the community

Offender's Background — Upper-class family, loss of parents, one sibling, highly structured childhood, above-average education, no historical substance abuse, parents had her assessed at various institutions

Details of the Crime — Location and tools are prepared before the attack. The victim is chosen, not at random, observed prior. Once at the site the victim is subdued, stripped of clothing, restrained for the purpose of earned punishment. Victims are castrated, genitals and limbs removed, internal organs removed, strangled, left to bleed to death. Once the victim is dead, the offender will carve the body and leave in a posed position. The remaining body parts will be further dismembered and discarded. The offender does exit the location with the victim's body parts.

Start counting, little Mary. You know from your gift that I keep much of them.

"Hale, your first profile... Was it released?" I asked. "This smacks of your first profile."

"Not to the public, but within the departments, yes," he answered.

"The offender identifies as female. They are close enough to one of us to have access to our interoffice documents. We need to tighten up shop." I motioned to the profile in my hands. "Time to release a profile from the killer."

"Release this?" Hale asked. "This isn't a profile. This looks like an application to a padded room."

"We're going to tweak it a little to call the offender out into the open." I nodded. "We also need to go back thirty or so years and start digging up old files on the building we were in when it was an asylum. We may find a few answers there."

"I'm on it," Hale responded. "Are you sure this little cat-and-mouse game isn't going to cause the perp to lash out?"

"Hale, the offender is going to kill, regardless of what we do. We need them to slip up, get cocky. We need some fucking mistakes," I replied. "We need to take back the control. Right now, we're running around in circles, picking up fucking body parts."

"Get it to me by tomorrow morning. I hope you're right, Grant. I fucking pray you're right." Hale groaned, rubbing the bridge of his nose.

"So do I," I answered. "I'm so fucking sick of living in this wound, Hale. I need out and this may be the only way."

Hale touched my hand and ran his fingers over my knuckles. "Whatever it takes, Mary. I'm there with you."

Chapter Thirteen

Saturday, December 10, 2016 — nine a.m.
One Police Plaza, New York
Mary

The janitor at One Police Plaza was quite a spindly person. I couldn't decide if his bones had grown faster than his flesh could keep up with or his skin had shrunk and his bones were threatening to tear through. He had the appearance of someone who should be lurking in a dark and dingy basement, waiting for bad little boys and girls. The curve of the raggedy old man's spine was like an under-watered flower. His limbs just sort of sagged. His shifty eyes were the palest of blue, like a creature that had spent his entire life in perpetual darkness. His movements were closer to slinking and leering, as if his body were too weighty to move in fluid motions.

The stubble on his chin looked like he had thought long and hard about bringing a blade to his throat. He would stop, nodding his head and darting his eyes from one side to the other side. Then he would smile in a way that made me notice the expression in his eyes. There was too much of him in there, an extra voice or two. There was something about him that made the tiny hairs on the back of my neck stand at attention. He paused every so many feet to laugh at something that only he could hear, his Adam's apple rubbing against his paper-thin skin. There was nothing creepier to me than a person with emotions that didn't match the situation, like someone smiling at a crime scene, laughing when others were in pain, unable to truly look sad. Children could be this way, but seeing it in an adult was disturbing.

"You all may want to search his basement," I whispered to Hale, only half joking.

He smiled. "I was just making a mental note to talk to someone about the importance of background checks and medical clearances."

I paced in the hall, waiting to present the profile to the dozens of reporters. My anxiety had punched me in the stomach while I waited. Usually, when my stress or anxiety was this high, I'd cry. I couldn't help it. It was my release. Crying was how I understood my emotions and myself best. It let me know who I was deep inside. It was my strength and my weakness. But when I was on a case, I wished I could turn my tears off. I've learned how to save them for when I was alone. Counting to ten, deep breathing, and I managed to dam off my tear ducts. They would burn until I finally let it out.

When it was go time, I wanted to puke. I stood at the front of the room on a small raised stage with an old wooden podium in the front middle. Microphones waited for us to give a profile of The Nursey Killer. The room was filled, standing room only, with enquiring minds and curious cops. Hale took to the podium with a pre-written speech I had provided to him this morning.

I watched the reporters swirling in a frenzy. They were excited. I couldn't understand, for the life of me, how they could be so thrilled over death and carnage. The news had stopped being 'the news' years ago. Now it was about ratings, money, popularity and population control. It reminded me more of a puppet show than journalism. The stations and social media gobbled up the worst of the worst. The more violence, blood and gore, the better it played out on television. We would use this shitshow to our advantage. The media wasn't journalism anymore. I hated it, but this time, I'd use it to my advantage. The stations wolfed down each word like a ravenous pup, thrilled at the prospect of higher ratings. Ratings meant money, and money made the world go around. I wondered for a moment when the media would bring back the gladiator rings. You couldn't buy a rating like that. Humanity was against atrocities, but mankind would watch, and in secret, would love every minute of it. It was who we were conditioned to be. We all belonged to a secret society built on the love of someone else's failures and horrors. If it wasn't happening to us, it was all good. Morality was for losers. Winners were the ones who 'pushed the envelope'.

Hale stood at the podium. He commanded attention. He silenced the room with one look. Every inch of him said, 'I don't fuck around.' Watching him take control made me shiver. It was a turn on. I reprimanded myself for thinking that at a time like this. I also forgave myself for my very human instincts.

"We suspect that someone in this community knows this individual. You will have spoken to them, met for coffee, jogged the same trails, shopped at the same stores. We are searching for anyone who is particularly interested in this case or the media coverage, someone who has had unusual behaviors since mid-November — extended breaks from work, changes in habits. We want this information. We are asking for the community's support once again to help us gather new leads and new information to bring this to a conclusion. We will provide you with our tip line numbers at the end of today. Again, we feel that someone in the community knows this offender well enough to notice these small variations in their behavior." Hale spoke first. He extended his hand to me. "Dr. Mary Grant will be providing a profile on the offender."

I stepped forward and cleared my throat. "The offender is an adult female, approximately forty years of age, does not have children or the ability for children. She targets those who have what she desires — a family. She has no outstanding physical features, medium to heavy in stature, harmless appearance, poorly educated, transient lifestyle, divorced, no close family ties, no interpersonal relationships, no community ties, unremarkable and does not stand out in the community. The offender was sexually abused as a child then abandoned into the system. She has no preference to the sex or ethnicity of her victims, however, she believes she is doing the job of the authorities. This offender has an extensive criminal background — sex-trade work and unassociated offenses." I read from my notes, feeling the eyes of the world staring back at me. I knew the offender would see me, and my words would anger them. This would be a kick to their ego. "I urge the public not to approach the offender. This individual is highly dangerous, suffering from extreme psychosis, is not medicated and will attack out of fear. We have time for a few questions. A complete profile will be made available."

Hands flew into the air. Hale approached the podium and pointed to the first reporter. I backed up and waited. The profile I had worked up wasn't far from my honest thoughts. After spending the night pouring over the evidence, letters, wording and how each victim was killed, I would bet the farm on my profile. A female sociopath. Rarer than a male, but not rare enough to ignore it. Throughout history there have been many female serial killers. It just isn't often they are brought up in conversation when we talk about killers.

Hale leaned into my ear when we stepped out. "We've just opened a three-ringed circus."

Special Agent Morgan Ridley jogged up the hall, holding a file. "We've narrowed it down to just over eighty admitted to the old New York Asylum for the Insane."

He handed the file to me, bypassing Hale. I grinned.

"Do I not work here anymore?" Hale asked.

I pulled half the papers and passed them over. "Divide and conquer."

It would be a long day and night. We'd be digging through archives and seeing who was still alive, who was out on the streets and who would be capable of serial murders. Not everyone who was clinically insane was capable of murder and not every murderer was clinically insane. This was the first substantial lead we'd had until the phones lit up with everyone suspecting their neighbor.

We would wait for the next letter to be delivered to the newspapers and pray there would be a fingerprint, fibers or the smallest of clues. I knew, no matter what I said to the media, the killer would strike again. It didn't matter what route we took. If we pumped up their ego, they would thrill-kill. If we insulted them, they would rage-kill. If we were neutral, they would kill for more attention. Or, they would continue on the path they were on, and nothing we did or said would interrupt it.

I stepped away from Hale. "Dinner at Sal's, for old time's sake?"

Hale grinned from ear to ear. I didn't have to ask him twice. "Is this your way of asking me out on a date? How very unprofessional of you — and in front of my colleagues?"

I rolled my eyes. "You could be eating alone if you keep it up?"

"For the record, my nanna thinks I'm a catch," Hale countered and followed me out.

"I thought you didn't have any family?" I asked.

Hale shrugged. "If I did, I'm sure she'd tell you that I'm a catch."

"Move it, lover boy," I said and nudged him to follow me out. I knew the wall between us that separated personal and professional was teetering on one small brick. Soon, the brick would crumble and the wall would be rubble at our feet. I should have cared more than I did.

Chapter Fourteen

Sunday, December 11, 2016
New York, New York
Received and printed by The Daily News

Letters from a deranged mind,

I watched you at the Riverside, high-fiving each other over the sick fuck I strung up for you. I know how happy it made you. I took a child rapist off the streets. You're welcome. Trust me. That sick piece of shit got less than what he deserved. Sadly, I was running out of time. I am always running late. But you know how that goes. Tick, tock, we are always on the clock. We have more in common than you think. We're both on the side of justice. I just take a different route – the road less traveled. I am on the road you want to walk down but fear the consequences. I do not fear them. I fear very little.

I saw you on the news and read my profile. Should I be honored or insulted? You're so pathetic it's almost tragic. You are all a fucking pathetic waste of skin. You don't know me. You don't know a fucking thing about me. Abused by my *father? Ha! No, I wasn't. Below average IQ? I believe mine to be rather high. Not unless you're lumping me into the category that includes the ridiculous men and women who stand on their soap boxes screaming for change while being blown by hookers and going home to kick their kids. That, I would consider an insult. Are you insulting me? Do we need to meet to set the record straight? I'd like that. I'd like to meet you. We can play. Do you want to? I have so many delightful games we can play. We can start with Twenty Questions. I'll go first. Tell me your greatest fear. I bet I can guess. Is it...failure? No. You've seen failure many times. Is it...loneliness? No, you've faced that when I took Henry and painted the town red with him. Perhaps it is waking up and hearing the voice of Mother dearest and the shuffling footfalls of Father?* **Bingo!** *Winner, winner, chicken dinner! You're a joke, but what can one expect from civil servants? A few grand, a slip of paper on the wall and all of a sudden you're an expert? You're part of the problem, not the solution.*

Why are you so afraid of me? You're scared. Why? What did I do to you? Oh! It's the fear of mental illness and the killing your loved ones' thing, right? You think I'm gonna come back and kill the survivors? If I wanted them dead, they would be dead. End of fucking story. I would have killed them at the same time. I'm a pacifist. I never hurt anyone who didn't deserve it. I don't have a criminal record, even though you said I probably do. But no! Why would you say I would? Just a stab in the fucking dark? Take it from me. You don't want to be stabbing around in the dark. It really takes the fun out of things.

You have made me angry again. I think you should leave now, Mary. You should go far away and not come back. Though, to be honest, I'm not sure why you're here, anyway. The angrier I get, the more you will feel it without me laying one finger on your head. You're trying to make me leave. Let's see who fucking leaves.

For the record, I don't have a mental illness at all. Perhaps I lose my cool every now and again. Well, not this bit, but the early parts for sure. I was a little crazed, but now? No. This is a journey for us all, and I'll thank you to keep your artistic shame to yourself. This is how I ensure we all wake up. If there is no guide like me to help them, everyone will remain blind. It is a baptism of fire. That is the only way. You are like everyone else, shoving down horse pills, licking the balls of the big pharma. You are their guinea pig. I won't dare swallow it down dose by dose, being analyzed and poked at for my attempts at a transformation and ridding the world of crusted scum. You won't make it. And at the end of this, I will be on top. Just wait.

Put your needles away. I'm not done playing. Not even close. The chase is only a sport for me, but I know it means everything to you. For me, ending your life is just a small part of a bigger plan. All your life you've been told that victory is assured for your side. It is, of course, bullshit. You live in a box of lies and darkness, under the illusion of light and goodness – but no more. There is no more hope. There will be no rescue. It's just me and you, puppet of mine. You aren't a hero, Mary. You are nothing. You are less than a cold drop of rain on the scorched earth. The chase is on, my dear Mary. I will find you, and we will have such fun together. I will hunt you down like the vermin we both know you are. I will exterminate everyone close to you for your lesson. All lessons are learned in the hardest of ways. Isn't that what your daddy always told you? You can't run from me forever. You are already in my crosshairs. I have a knife just for you. You're going to love it.

So run, little Mary. Run as fast as your feet can take you. Hide. I do love me a game of hide and seek. I will find you and do to you what I do best, teach lessons to young boys and girls. I promise you death, release from this world – the world that's taken who you are and twisted it into something you will be punished for, a liar.

I will meditate on your annihilation and the cold leap of joy that I will feel when the light is extinguished from your eyes. What I cannot exploit, I will destroy. Is your pulse hammering yet? Your daddy isn't the only one who keeps his promises. I promise to punish you in ways you haven't felt since your father took off his belt. You should have switched sides when I offered you the chance.

Until we meet.

Your friend always, TNK

* * * *

Brock

I hadn't met a more courageous woman than Mary. She took each hit and kept on going. But now we waited. We were hanging on for a clue that I feared would never come. This had turned from a mission for the masses into a mission for Mary. I wanted her to have peace, to heal. And with this SOB out there that would never happen. Even if she moved on from me, I still wanted her to be able to move on, period.

"How are you holding up?" I asked her, cradling the phone between my ear and shoulder.

I was one floor under her in bed. I knew she was in bed above me. I had heard her shuffling around. It took sheer will to keep me from knocking on her door and trying to hold her in my arms.

"I'm good. I'm tired, but doing all right. How about you?" Mary asked.

Her concern for me was touching. "Same, I'm tired. I think we're all running on determination spiked with espresso beans."

It was good to hear her voice. I depended on it daily. She had turned into the driving force behind my willingness to get out of bed and face the day. But she had also turned into my constant worry. Every noise I heard in the room above me stirred me out of a dead sleep. I would listen to her pace and shower for an hour, only to pace some more. She rarely slept, and when she did, I could hear her toss and turn.

"We don't have much time left, Hale," Mary whispered. I caught the fear and pain in her voice. "I can't think of not catching TNK, but what if we don't? This will play out again in a year. I don't think I have it in me to do this again."

"We'll catch 'em, Mary. I personally know half of the team on the ground working this case. The best of the best is in New York, combing the streets. Have faith, Mary."

She sighed. "I don't doubt the brilliance of your team, Hale. I doubt TNK will make the mistakes we need her to make for us to find her."

"As you've said time and time again, no one is perfect. Everyone makes mistakes. We just have to look closer. We have to stay on our toes."

I didn't know what else to say. I didn't want to tell Mary that I agreed with her or that I didn't think we'd find the bastard, no matter how many men we had on the ground. If TNK didn't fuck up, we were screwed.

"Breakfast in the morning?" I asked.

"Only if you're buying," she joked. Her little touch of laughter made my body relax.

"It's a date, a professional one. We can call it a business meeting," I joked back and said goodnight.

"It's a date. Goodnight, Hale," she replied and hung up.

I slid my phone onto my nightstand. If I couldn't see her, I had to hear her voice before I slept. It was the only thing that helped me sleep at night. She was not the only one battling monsters. My nightmares had stepped up a few notches since I'd learned Mary was the target. I wouldn't make it out of this if she fell into the hands of TNK. I'd burn the city to the ground to find the sick fuck and nothing, short of my own death, would keep me from torturing TNK until the most gruesome death in history.

Chapter Fifteen

Friday, December 16, 2016 — nine a.m.
One Police Plaza, New York
Crime Scene Three
Verse Three — With silver bells and cockleshells
Mary

The white church had been a pillar of the community during its time. It still had followers, but nothing like what its attendance had been before people realized they wouldn't burst into flames for sin. The building stood tall and firm, white with gold and stained glass. What stood out were not the little gargoyles or the millions of dollars poured into the building, but the human heart nailed to the front door. That was bound to catch attention, and it did. A jogger had called it in thirty minutes before we'd arrived at four. The jogger was being questioned, their background checked and she would be held until we were one hundred percent sure she wasn't our offender. Until we had the bad guy in cuffs, that jogger's life was about to be turned upside down.

Gnarled trees hung low over the impressive church, dragging branches around the siding in the winter winds. The police lights added to the heaviness in the air. We all could feel it. This was the third verse in the rhyme, one more and we would lose our chance at catching the son of a bitch who was responsible. She would disappear for another year where we would have to start from scratch. The threat of losing our chance had pressed heavily on our shoulders with every breath we took, like the weight of the world was resting upon us. The pressure didn't help. It made me feel sick, not motivated.

I leaned against a black SUV with Hale, sipping our coffee, craving one last boost of energy. Neither of us had been to sleep yet, nor had we gotten our breakfast. As the saying went, 'we'd sleep when we were dead'. At this rate, it wouldn't be that far off. We had been pushing ourselves too hard, and I could feel it in my bones. I had tried to sleep, but each night was a futile attempt to win over my mind. I wasn't ready to start the cycle again in the morning. I would wake up and fight against the day, only to drop dead in bed with nightmares. For a moment, I wondered if mankind had always been this way, the price we paid for modern lifestyles and ignorance of our health and sanity. Either way, sleep or no sleep, it sucked. 'Tired until retired' — now there was a slogan to see me through the next two decades.

"I'm tired as hell. I could easily pull off being a walking zombie, dead on the inside but subconsciously awake," Hale muttered. He rotated his shoulders and set his cup down. "Any more coffee and I'll piss a Venti."

"It's the best part of waking up." I smiled.

"True, for those in the world who are just waking up. I've been awake for almost thirty-five hours straight."

"Ahh, the glamorous life of a special agent. They should put that in their ads," I replied and set my coffee down. "Ready? They haven't entered the scene yet. They're waiting for us to somehow work our magic and find a clue."

"I'm never fucking ready for this shit," Hale answered and pulled on a set of gloves.

From the icy road, I followed Hale through the parking lot to the front door. Drips of now-frozen blood pooled on the ground on the front steps, like little red skating arenas. The massive oak doors were wide open. Walking through them made me shiver. I wasn't a fan of organized religion. Just being there was uncomfortable. The entrance was like every other church I had seen. Small oak bookshelves lined the broad walls, and a polished wooden floor led to another set of doors. This was probably what hell was like, room after room, waiting to pay.

Inside the second set of doors we were blasted with sticky heat. It was enough to make you want to take off the layers of winter clothes.

"This must be what hell feels like," Hale whispered to me.

I grinned. "I was just thinking the same thing."

Hale stepped to the side of the aisle. Ahead of him stood an altar, polished like the floor. Two nude, male bodies dangled over the front stage from the rafters. The flickering lights from outside flickered through the stained-glass windows, casting an eerie glow over the scene. I paused and took it all in. I scanned the room. We started at the rear and worked our way forward. Each inch of the church was searched for anything that shouldn't be there.

"Hale," I called out, pointing at a pew, fourth from the back. A long dark hair lay on the wooden bench. Not unusual, but for a place as clean as this, it stood out like a sore thumb. It could be the cleaning crew or it could be from the killer, who had perhaps sat and observed their masterpiece.

Hale placed an evidence marker, took pictures and bagged the hair. We pressed forward. It wasn't until we stood ten feet from the bodies that we found a print. Hale kneeled and stared at the floor. I didn't see it until he positioned his light at an angle. I rested my foot beside it and he took pictures. It was roughly an inch bigger than my size eight, but not as wide as mine. Hale lifted the shoe print and packaged it.

I frowned. "Is it me or was this too easy? Never has the offender left evidence, but today, we find a hair *and* a shoe print?"

"Didn't you say the killer would make mistakes?"

I nodded. "I did, but these aren't mistakes, Hale. A hair seamlessly positioned? A shoe print impeccably placed? Those aren't mistakes. Something about this doesn't sit right. My guess is that the hair and shoe belong to a soon-to-be vic or a previous one. It's a big 'fuck you' from the killer."

"Then we press on, Grant. It's all we can do," Hale said and brought our attention to the first victim hanging from the rafters. "Jesus Christ."

I glanced up and had to turn away. My stomach rolled with the urge to bring up the only thing I had consumed in days, coffee. I breathed in deeply and could taste the vic's charred flesh and scorched hair. I turned back with my hand over my nose. It wasn't that the skin on his body was burned in random places. It had been seared off completely. From the scorch marks on the semi-cooked muscle beneath, it appeared like it had been done with a blow torch, a little at a time. He dangled with his arms over his head. Every inch of his skin had been charred down to the muscle. One slash across the abdomen had exposed his intestines, which were used to string him up. Thumbscrews held his thumbs together.

"Silver bells," I whispered. Thumb screws were thought to signify silver bells, in the rhyme.

The ribcage had been cracked and pried open. The whiteness of the bone stood out from the sea of flesh. The heart had been cleaved from his body, now nailed to the front door. Chunks of muscle had been cut back and pinned with iron nails banged in.

"The mouth isn't gagged. Maybe the killer enjoyed the screams," Hale mentioned.

I nodded. "Perhaps, but how do you kill someone in this fashion without the entire city block hearing something? You can't burn a man to death without someone noticing. He wasn't conscious during this. There would be no way this was done in complete silence while he was awake."

This took time, energy, strength. We moved to the second man and Hale puked on the floor.

"What the fuck is that?" Hale asked, pointing to the victim's genitalia.

"Cockleshells," I answered. "They are genital torture devices designed to crush the penis."

I scanned the front of the church and stepped around the hanging bodies to the polished podium and looked out over the church. On the podium sat a small white card.

With silver bells and cockleshells.

I turned my back on the scene. I needed out. I needed the air in my lungs to no longer taste of burning men. This, by far, was the worst thing I had ever seen. This topped the charts of a hundred and one reasons I would never sleep again. Hale followed behind me, motioning for the police to come in and start processing the scene. We weren't going to find anything more than nightmares within those walls.

I stopped on the front steps and eyed up the gargoyles, little monsters in stone. I was almost jealous of their lack of emotion, frozen in time where all of humanity's disgust and rage couldn't touch them. They were the faces of time stood still, never to know love and hate. What a mercy it must be for a monster to be frozen like that. I wondered why the men had been strung up in a church. Perhaps to show that extinguishing the cruelty was a positive thing? There could be no guilt in killing the tyrants of our nightmares. Had these men been offenders? Was the killer hunting the silent criminals, roaming bad guys we had yet to catch?

I took a seat on the frozen ground and breathed deeply, going over the profile in my head. Each time I thought I had the killer pegged, something else had come to light, and I wasn't ready for the curveball. I felt like it had slammed into my chest and I was left scrambling. I turned to face the church, scanning the grounds and street. The offender knew they wouldn't be caught. They had scoped out the area and knew the exact times the roads would be free and clear.

The tall, iron gate surrounding the property gave no cover. The winter had taken the leaves from the trees, removing any options for concealment, had someone jogged past. Living in a day and age where no one stopped to ask questions made the perfect setting for a killer to walk down the road in broad daylight, covered in blood, holding a severed head. I scanned the street, darkness at one end, lights and the city that never slept at the other. The offender had come from the darkness. They weren't stupid enough to risk getting caught, no matter how blind people had grown out of fear of being a second severed head.

There were dozens of footprints in the snow, but I knew none would belong to the offender. The only trace they had ever left was sitting inside the church. It tugged at my gut instinct. Nothing was right about it. People made mistakes, but not effortlessly placed mistakes. Whoever had owned that hair likely had nothing to do with the crime. Whoever was strung up inside had something to do with me. I could feel it, like walking into a familiar room and not remembering when you had been there before.

"Penny for your thoughts," Hale said and dropped down beside me on the curb.

"I'm wondering who the victims are," I answered, "if I cared about them, if they were friends or if they were just some random men I had crossed paths with. Either way, I feel sick knowing they died because they knew me in some way."

Hale pulled an evidence bag. "They found the belongings of one of the men. His name is Charles Cavanaugh. Mean anything to you?"

I nodded. "We're not close. He's an intern in my department. Nice enough guy, but I'm pretty sure he was high every time we spoke. He was going to be coming to London during my next seminar at Scotland Yard. I think he and April had a thing they were trying to hide."

"We'll run the evidence and see what turns up. I'm taking a day off. You should, too," Hale said and stood. He held out his hand and helped me stand. "You look like shit, Grant. Get some rest."

"Gee, thanks, Hale. You sure have a way with the ladies," I countered.

He winked. "It worked on you, didn't it?"

I rolled my eyes at him.

His smile widened. "I don't want this to insult you, but you're not one of the ladies. You're one of us."

I smiled. I took it as a compliment, the way it had been meant. To be considered 'one of the guys' had meant respect, nothing less. I waved him off and caught a ride with a civvie. I would call in later in the day for an update on the hair and shoe print. I didn't hold out hope that it would bring us closer to catching the sick SOB, but a shred of hope was still there. The problem with hope? It can lead to desperation. We were almost there, almost desperate.

Chapter Sixteen

Sunday, December 18, 2016
New York
Received and printed by The Washington Square News

Letters from a deranged mind,
You have pretty eyes. I like the way they sparkle. It reminds me of freshly spilled blood over rocks. I want to keep them for all days. I want to hold them in my hands at night. I want them to sit on my nightstand and watch me while I masturbate. I want to dip them in my fluids and lick them clean, so you remain sparkling. Why do you turn away when I look at you? Why don't you like to make eye contact? Why do you stare at me like I'm not real? You are not real. Get out of my head. Stay away from me. All of you stay the fuck away from me. I was nice to you. I loved you all. Why do you hate me? What have I done to you? Nothing.
I think I scare you because I don't wrap my words in sugary cow shit. Perhaps if I wrapped it in pretty pink paper, you'd be less fearful of my truths. I will wrap my truths in your hair, ripped from your head, so they are familiar to you.

Your little head is filled with ugly little lies. Maybe if my words were somewhere in between lunatic and god-worship, you'd like me more, like the churches and priests and people who take your money and lie to your face. Maybe if I started robbing you, too, you'd think more of me. Would you? Would it help if I took more from you? I thought taking a life was enough, but perhaps I should rip the earrings from your ears and cut the rings from your fingers. You're all puppets. You fucking disgust me.

With silver bells and cockleshells... Did you like that, Mary? Did it make you grin? It made me smile. I had so many ideas for this one. Did you like my final piece? It was perfect, all of it. Did it bother you to know them? Does it sadden you to see his face? I knew it would mean more to you if you knew them. All of this is for you. You should have left when I told you to, but you never listen. Do you, Mary? Don't cry for them. They deserved it. He burned, like hell on Earth. The church was fitting. Don't you agree? They made me go to church as if I had reason to repent. I do not feel sincere regret or remorse.

Do you want to sit me down and let you pick my brain apart like I pick everyone else apart? Or ask me about my childhood? Did Daddy like to touch me? Did Mommy like to whip me?

My mental functioning is excellent. The shrinks with their clipboards and judgment don't scare me. They can drop their pens and put their needles away. You can find me if you really wanted to. If you think hard enough and long enough, you will find me kicked back on a sofa, covered in blood, licking my fingers clean. If you wanted me off the streets, you could have taken me out many times. You haven't looked hard enough. You're lazy, all of you. You sit on your fat asses while I am free. Now you tell me, who is to blame for me running your streets and treating your homes like my personal amusement park? Not I, I will not take responsibility for your own inaction.

One more verse. It will be my last. You have one more chance to catch me, then I am gone. Maybe for good or maybe just for another year. I haven't decided. Retirement does sound good, but so does slaughtering an entire city. I can't do both. Decisions, decisions. This reminds me of something, my Mary. Do I go left or do I go right? It appears we have come almost full circle. Stop me before I create an infinity, I may never stop then.

Put your pills away, Mary, I won't be needing them. You can't cure sanity. You can't medicate someone who is completely sane. That's the beauty of this. That's what scares you most. You can't cure me of being reasonable. You, on the other hand, look like you are losing a battle with sanity. Mary, are you going to break again? Can you almost taste those pills again? Do you need help? Let me help you, Mary. Let me put you out of your misery. I would be honored. I would go away for all time, satisfied that my life's work has been complete. I'd have forced you all to see that the monsters aren't just under your bed. They are lurking around every corner. Your death would complete the circle. It would prove my point. Will you do this for mankind? Or are you as selfish as the next sniveling little cunt?

Until we meet.
Your friend always, TNK

* * * *

Brock

Mary and I sat in the bar, reading the newest letter in the newspaper. Neither of us had much steam left. We were run down and exhausted, traipsing around the city and face-planting into brick walls. It was coming down to the wire. Time was running out. We all knew it, but no one wanted to say it out loud. With few words exchanged between us, we had a few drinks then headed up in the elevator.

"I miss you," Mary whispered, turning to face me. She touched my hand.

"I miss you, too," I answered.

Without warning, she launched herself into my arms, slamming her lips into mine, and it nearly knocked the wind out of me. I hadn't a single moment to react before she pushed her tongue between my lips and, at my willingness to open my mouth, she kissed me from the inside out. I roamed my hands over her body, greedy and hurried. She arched her body up into my chest. Her moans filled my mouth. She brushed her lips across mine when I gripped her breast, feeling her rock-hard nipple through her silk blouse. I knew I should have pulled away, but I lost myself in her. In the tiny moments we had in the elevator, my mind and senses got caught up in her taste.

"Hale," she whispered, prolonging each letter as if each one brought her pleasure.

I grinned. Never had my name ever sounded so erotic. From the first time we had kissed, my brain had been lit on fire, and I had been hooked on her taste. Having her in my arms had eased a tension I hadn't known I had been carrying on my shoulders. I couldn't bear the thought of never touching her again, of her never being safe against me again. Yet, I could barely breathe when she was around, and I struggled harder for air when she wasn't. She was my deliverance and my torment. I lived for both. I knew that if I lost her, I would lose myself.

The elevator opened, and she stepped out, turning with a wink. The doors closed, and my back hit the wall of the little metal box that had handed me a gift, another moment with Mary. That kiss had obliterated every horrible thought. For the first time since seeing her again, my mind was locked into the present. Drunk on endorphins, my only desire was to feel her one more time, to move my hands over her body and softness and make her call out my name. A kiss like that was a beginning, a promise of much more to come. For the briefest of moments it had taken for us to head up to her floor, I had Mary back. I would do whatever it took to keep her.

I showered with a grin on my face. That kiss had given me hope. It was a promise that maybe shit would work out and I'd get a chance at something better. In my line of work, I needed a piece of goodness to come home to, to drown out the horror of mankind.

The ding on my phone made my pulse race. A text from Mary.

Are you going to open your door or should I stand here all night?

I dropped my phone and unlocked my door. Mary didn't wait to be invited in. She pushed open the door and shut it behind her. She grabbed my shoulders and pulled me to her mouth. I lifted her onto my toweled hips and carried her to my bed. No words were exchanged. She lifted off her shirt, and I helped take off her pants. She shoved me to my knees, leaned back onto her elbows and spread her legs.

"Please. I need this tonight." Her voice was throaty.

I lifted her thighs to my shoulders and pressed my lips to her center. I didn't waste another minute. I sucked on her clit and moved her hips against my mouth. She tasted better than I had remembered. There was a sweetness to her that I couldn't get enough of. I wanted to drink her down to the last drop. It didn't take long for her to grab my hair and moan my name. I kept my mouth firmly in place and drank her orgasm.

"Fuck me," Mary groaned.

Mary tugged at my arms until I dropped her thighs. She reached into her pants and returned with a condom. Mary had come prepared. I kneeled between her legs and rolled it on. I leaned into her and kissed her while I worked myself inside her. I paused for a heartbeat. I loved the moment when I first entered her – tight, warm, wet. It was perfect. I made slow and deliberate strokes over her sweet spot. I knew her body inside and out. She tossed back her head and moaned my name. I drew it out, every second. I wanted it to last forever. Nothing else in the world mattered at that moment. It was just her and me – no pain, no work, no sadness.

When we both were sated, she didn't bolt like I had thought she would. She lifted my arms around her and curled into me.

"For one night, please?" Mary asked. "I need to feel something more than terror."

"For as long as you want," I replied and hoped it would be for all days.

Mary fell asleep fast. I glanced at her calm face while she slept. This had been the first time I had seen her without worry lines engraved on her face. She seemed peaceful for once. As I watched her, a thought popped into my mind. *I could get used to waking up beside her.*

What surprised me most was that it wasn't followed up with panic about giving up my single life. That shouldn't bother me. Single life only seemed fun in the movies. Even though I hadn't known her for very long, it felt like we'd been through hell and back, together. I knew in my heart that she was now a part of my life. Whether it would be my past or my future was still up for debate.

"I love you," I whispered and kissed her temple. Mary in my arms felt right, honest.

Chapter Seventeen

Tuesday, December 20, 2016 — eleven a.m.
One Police Plaza, New York
Mary

The interview room at One Police Plaza was tasteful in a corporate way. Nothing remarkable enough to cause offense, no matter what a person's preferences might have been. It was small and square with four metal chairs and a metal table. There was no back wall to the interview room, only tempered glass, cracked and scuffed from years of abuse. The walls were gray and faded. You could almost see the concrete through the fifteen-year-old paint job. The rear wall held a small barred window let in the slightest of light, lost in the shadows of the room. It looked like every other interview room. They didn't call them interrogation rooms anymore. Apparently it was too presumptuous and implied guilt.

I sat on the other side of the glass, away from the crazies who had climbed out of the woodwork and claimed to be The Nursey Killer. The lines had been going nonstop since the profile had been released. The front doors of every cop shop in town had been a revolving door for insanity. For every one thousand tips, we had perhaps one lead, all of which had amounted to overtime and wasted man hours.

I pulled up a chair beside Hale. I was immediately uncomfortable. My mouth was dry, and my throat felt like sandpaper. I had woken with Hale wrapped around me. I hadn't wanted to move. I'd felt safe and I'd wanted to stay in that moment forever. Instead, I'd got up and left him sleeping. Now, sitting beside him, I felt embarrassed about ducking out without saying a word. I held a small stack of files from the old asylum. Sitting around watching interviews was a waste of time and made my skin itch with unease.

"Hale, why the hell are we just sitting here?" I finally asked.

"Well, good morning to you." Hale pointed to the window. "This one… I wanted you to see this one. She says she knows who the killer is. I think you ought to take a listen."

Hale punched a small black button and the once-silent room filled with the shaky voice of another addiction victim. The waiting room was brimming with those who had fallen. The statistics counted broken souls like dollar bills. Each dollar bill was a person, a tragedy, a castaway. Seeing the scrawny woman fidget, picking at her face and arms, made me turn away. I couldn't face seeing what road any one of us could have chosen, including me.

"Her name is Delphine," the small-framed woman spoke. Her hands were visible of fresh track marks when she gripped a white Styrofoam coffee cup. "She's crazy, but not in the way you say she is. She talks to herself then answers herself like someone else is there that isn't. She's been squatting in the old buildings down by the river where they found that dead guy in the spiderweb. She left last night. She said she had a meeting with a doctor — Grant or something like that. She told me that she knows her and has a score to settle with her. Said she was screwed over by Grant's dad a long time ago."

My mouth dropped open, and I leaned in, staring.

"She said Grant wants to put her in the loony bin. I can see why. She's fucking crazy. She killed my cat because I thought she was talking to herself again but she was talking to me. When I wasn't listening, she offed my pet. Said I had to learn some manners."

"Can you tell me what Delphine looks like?" the officer in the room asked.

"Long brown hair, really nice hair for someone who don't have no home. She's my height but doesn't seem like she's gone without a meal. She dresses nicer, too. I haven't seen her do any drugs, but she probably should be on some to calm her down. Once, I took a pair of her runners and she tried to cut my feet off."

The officer turned to the window then back to the woman. "What size are your feet?"

"Just over eight. I didn't keep the shoes. They were too tight, but she wouldn't listen," she answered.

Hale clicked off the speaker. "Sounds legit."

I stood. "Let's move it."

"Already sent a team over, no sign of the perp," he answered. "Do you know anyone who may hold a grudge against your family, someone who has been institutionalized?"

"Not in particular, but I've sent many, myself. It's what I do, Hale," I answered. I lifted the stack of files. "We can start here. I was born and raised in New York, as were my parents. If it is someone who was sent away at a young age, they're in here."

"Worth a shot. Anyone by the name of Delphine?" he asked, and I shook my head. "Didn't think it would be that easy."

On the drive to visit the first name in the files, Carol Tate, I gave him a preview of each file. I had narrowed it down to just over twenty. All but five had killed themselves. All five had been institutionalized for various mental health conditions, all severe and all fit the profile of budding psychopaths.

Carol Tate lived in a small bachelor suite in the shady part of town. Carol answered the door by way of opening it one inch and not removing the chain lock. The file said she was thirty-nine, but she appeared closer to sixty. Her mental illness had wrapped its greedy fingers around her throat and had been choking the life out of her ever since. Her thin and starved frame could almost fit through that one-inch gap. Her fingertips were chewed and peeling. Scabs covered the ends of each nail. Her file said she had an anxiety disorder. That was a slight understatement. Her darting eyes and quickened breathing said her anxiety was closer to being tied to an electric fence—not enough to kill her, but enough to keep her feeling constant distress.

"Sorry, wrong address," I said and stepped away from the door.

Hale followed me from the building. "You're not even going to question her?"

"Hale, does she seem like she could pull something like this off? Hell, I doubt she's left that apartment since the first day she moved in. She's probably capable of murder—we all are—but I seriously doubt she'd willingly leave her comfort zone to do anything more than grab her meds and maybe a bottle of booze."

"Who's next?" Hale asked. He looked back to the building once and nodded.

The second woman, Emily Easton, had every marker for a serial killer. Born into poverty and abused in every way a person could be, she'd spent twenty years in and out of institutions. She couldn't be around pets or small children or they would play her victim. Emily currently lived with relatives in an upscale district of New York. Her file said she was pumped up with enough medication to knock out an elephant or two. A home-care nurse administered the medication like clockwork. After five minutes at her door, we walked away. An ankle bracelet had been attached to Emily seven years ago, when she had been released from her last stint in a psych unit.

The third woman was being zipped into a body bag when we arrived. She had hung herself after writing on the walls in her own blood about the devil taking over her mind. I was pretty sure she wasn't the killer. She was too preoccupied with a different brand of crazy and had been institutionalized for three previous murders. Information didn't move between agencies with speed anymore, given she was dead and we were finding out alongside the neighbors.

The fourth woman wasn't home. Hale called it in, and she'd be found and brought in for questioning. The fifth, Yasmin Forrester, was out of the house at work. Her boyfriend, Aaron, knew about her mental health conditions and was more than happy to have us come in. It felt odd. He was odd. I wondered for a moment what *his* diagnosis was.

"She's home every evening after work. She works up at Marks Accounting firm, top floor. She takes medication three times a day. She says we must always be accountable for ourselves," he said, passing us a recent photo of Yasmin.

Her parents had both been killed in an accident, years ago. Police had suspected Yasmin but could never prove it. Yasmin was a petite woman with dirty blonde hair, and she looked like a bump in the night would send her back to the hospital. I scanned her apartment. Spotless. The books on her shelves were placed in alphabetical order and were all on topics of serial killers, murder, biographies of killers... It was a tribute to who she wanted to become, who she yearned to be.

"Yasmin is very open about her condition. She runs a group over at St. Mary's for those suffering from a brain illness," he added. "She sees her therapist twice a week and goes for regular reviews every six months. When she feels off, she makes a doctor's appointment to have her meds reviewed. She's proactive in her well-being. She's helped keep me on the straight and narrow."

Hale opened his notebook. "Aaron, what is your diagnosis?"

"Anxiety and depression," he answered.

"And?" I asked.

"Borderline personality disorder," he explained.

I nodded. "Are you medicated? Seeking treatment?"

"Yes, Yasmin has helped me find a doctor. I also go to group and see a counselor once a week. Yasmin has been a huge help and inspiration to me. Without her, I'd still be on the streets, eating out of dumpsters. She found me and saved me. She taught me not to be ashamed of how I was created. She says I should be honest about who I am. With that honesty will come dignity."

I extended my hand. "Thank you for speaking with us, Aaron. I appreciate your honesty and willingness to talk to us. If we have any further questions, we will be in touch."

"I'll let Yasmin know you were here. Thank you for stopping by," Aaron said and closed the door behind us.

I nudged Hale. "We need to call it in. Something about this rubs me the wrong way. Did you see the artwork of famous killers in history and the books on her shelves? Who the hell owns over fifty books on serial killers? Hell, I don't even own that many and I play with the monsters every day."

Yasmin was being picked up from work and would be escorted to the station for questioning. She may not be our killer, but I was fairly sure she was a killer, either in the making or had offended already. She was a classic manipulator, a master at influence and deception. It wasn't enough for me to tag her as the killer, but it was plenty for me to be interested in meeting her. I didn't know what flavor of monster she was, but just the same, I couldn't help but want to put a stop to it.

I was lost in my thoughts, making notes and going over each scene in the back of my mind. I replayed every detail, right down to how my skin crawled. Hale didn't disrupt my process. He had gotten used to me going radio silent. He drove us back to One Police Plaza, the radio humming just loud enough to drain out the constant sound of traffic and irrational drivers.

Special Agent Cole Nelson met us at the front door. "Miss Forrester is in interview room three. Before you go in, I did a little digging. You need to take a look at this."

He handed me what appeared to be screenshots of various websites and social media sites. Yasmin Forrester was active on sites about killers, sociopaths, how-to murder sites and had a download history numbering in the hundreds on topics about The Nursey Killer. on the sites dedicated to egging on the killer, she happened to be the most active user.

"She's been asking TNK to take her under her wing. She has even offered up her partner for a sacrifice," Cole added.

I scanned the pages, searching for something to nail her with and had my 'ah-ha' moment. I passed the page to Hale. "She's been feeding the killer names — names of men and women who have been charged and let go of crimes against children, rape, abuses. She has given a list of her groups she runs — dozens of people who suffer from various psychological diagnoses. Names, addresses and schedules."

"Any of our vics on there?" Hale asked, reading the document.

"Not that I can see. It doesn't look like the killer responds," I answered and motioned forward. "Let's go have a little chit-chat with Miss Forrester."

Before going in, I watched her through the viewing window. I wanted to see her condition before I sat across from her. Yasmin Forrester was smaller in person. Her hair was still dirty blonde like the photo but would have been lighter had she showered regularly. It was clear that the apartment wasn't clean on her account. Her eyes were sunken and gray. She appeared exhausted, haunted. Her expression showed that she'd collected and bore tragically every wrongdoing that had rained down on her. Her face was too thin and gaunt. She seemed emaciated, starved. Her bare arms and legs were ashy and pale.

Yasmin sat on the chair, slightly rocking. It was not enough for most to notice it, but mannerisms were my thing. Her fingertips clutched at her black pencil skirt — clench and unclench, over and over. Her face had the traits of someone in distress, buckling under the strain. Every few seconds she would scratch at her ears and swat at the air as if there were bugs. She jerked her head to the window, staring through it at me. I knew she couldn't see me, but it was unnerving. Whatever the outcome of today, I'd request a psych review.

"Morgan, make sure you have a few officers on standby. If she loses it, we're going to need a little help," I said.

"Do you want psych here?" he asked, and I nodded.

Hale and I stepped into the room. When we approached her, her stress visibly grew.

"What's in your hands?" she demanded.

We both brought our hands up, showed her they were empty. "Nothing," I replied, smiling at her, using a gentle gaze to calm her.

"Why did you pull me out of work?" she asked, her shoulders rising with tension.

I pushed the pages in front of her for her to view. "We have a few questions, Miss Forrester."

She stared at them and tried to hide the snarl forming on her face. "Since when is it illegal to be online?"

"Being online is not illegal. What you do when you are online could be illegal," Hale answered. "You have been trying to contact The Nursey Killer and have supplied them with several names of people you'd like to have killed. That, Miss Forrester, is illegal. Did you make contact with the killer?"

"Yes, we're good friends," she answered, smiling a cocky grin. "I met her years ago, during one of my stays in the White Room Hotel."

The White Room Hotel was what people had called a check-in at a psych hospital. I smiled back and decided I should bait her a little. Part of me hoped I didn't push her over the edge into oblivion and the other part wanted her off her rocker and locked up. "I do not believe The Nursey Killer knows who you are, let alone is friends with you."

It didn't take long for that edge to turn into a dark precipice.

"Yes, I know her. You don't know. You don't know *anything*. She said she will consider our friendship. We have spoken many times until I asked her to kill Aaron, then she said I was fucking crazy. Me, crazy? I'm not crazy. Delphine is the crazy one. She told me she was saving me for last, to carve the sickness from my mind. She told me she didn't like my gifts." Yasmin screamed, spit dripping down her chin. She stood from the table and leaned forward in a power stance. "I brought her presents. I brought her parts of me. I've loved her since the first day we met, and this is the thanks I get?"

I stood and backed away from her. I grabbed Hale's shoulder and pulled him back with me. I had seen her go from zero to fifty with an eye twitch that trapped animals displayed in a matter of seconds. What was coming next would be a special treat. I could hear the pending violence in her voice, shaking and begging to be let out.

"Where did you bring them, the gifts?" I asked.

"Her apartment with the other crazies, the apartment of dead cats. She goes there when she's bored," she answered. "I want to go home now. I'm going home now. I must go home. Aaron needs to be reminded to take his medication."

I motioned to the window for Morgan to send in the officers and turned back to Yasmin. "You won't be going home this evening."

Yasmin lunged over the table, almost reaching me. Four uniforms swarmed into the room and took her to the floor.

"She said she'd protect me. She told me she'd help me," Yasmin screamed and squirmed on the ground.

Hale and I stepped out of the room. Hale turned to me, frowning. "She did help her, sort of."

"We need a list of everyone who was ever admitted with her—on her floor, anyone she spoke to, everything," I said when I flagged down Morgan. "Keep searching Yasmin's email, computer history, everything."

"That was it. The offender made sure not to leave any form of a trail. Nothing I can see, anyway. I've sent it up the chain. Hopefully, someone else can find something."

I sighed. "The offender probably reached out in person and not online—hand-delivered letters, phone calls, all in person. The killer may be off the charts with insanity, but they're not stupid or we'd have them by now. Send a team to Yasmin's home and turn it upside down. But, Morgan, be careful. The man there? He will have a meltdown over the mess. Bring psych with you."

"Got it," he said and jogged down the hall.

Hale and I went back to the files. It was all we had for now. And to be honest, I was happy to spend more time with Hale, even if it was because Yasmin had given us a lead. The offender had stayed at the same hospital with Yasmin at the same time. The list would be long, but not long enough for it to be a dead end.

Chapter Eighteen

Saturday, December 24, 2016
New York City
Received and printed by The Metro New York

Letters from a deranged mind,
Happy Christmas Eve!
The holiday season just ain't what it used to be, is it?
What with the suicides on the rise, the over-consumption of
drugs and spirits and the absolute fucking depressing fact
that most people cannot afford to give their children anything
more than another shitty memory. I love how people step over
the starved just so they can buy the latest gadget. When the
hell did we go wrong? When did we decide to put up a tree
and fill it with meaningless crap we don't need over the needs
of our poor? I watch the advertisements on television, about
how much happiness one could have if they spent their life
savings on filling a tree. It showed such perfect and smiling
people, all of them happy and attractive. Are people so
emotionally retarded that they will buy products just to
elevate themselves? Is there some underdeveloped part of

your brain thinking 'If I buy this, I'll be happy'? You are Neanderthals, trying to wear fancy bone necklaces and beating each other over the heads.

And you wonder why I carry this disgust? I watched a woman push an elderly lady out of her way and snatch a pair of gloves from her hands. Rest assured, I'm adding her to my naughty list. She will most definitely get a visit from bad Santa. I'll make sure she is wearing those gloves when I cut her fingers off. People like that are the reason we have children running gangs and injecting with dirty needles. People like that show our young how important it is not to give a shit, to take care of themselves because no one else will. I'm writing this while I sit outside her house. That's how dedicated I am to ridding mankind of people like this fucking useless waste of skin. She's wrapping the gloves with a smile on her face. Little does she know that all choices have consequences, and I am her consequence. Hunting her down doesn't make me crazy. Doing nothing about it does. Maybe if I were to say I was carrying out the word of God, you'd all be thanking me? We pay the church to hurt people. Perhaps I should be sending you all a bill?

If one should stand up with conviction and say they are an angel of mercy sent from God to save the sinners, they would end up in a white padded room, saliva dripping from their drugged-out mouth. Away with their ability to wear shoelaces or have anything else they could hang themselves with. But, if they were to say, 'I'm a priest. Come into my house of God and let us wash away your sins', they'd get a fucking tax break. If they were found somewhere in between raving lunatic and God worshipper, they'd be bombarded with the usual questions. How was your childhood? What kind of punishment did you receive growing up? Did Daddy like to touch you? Easy questions… Shit that I have learned to answer in my sleep. My mental functioning is not the question. The shrinks will need to pester someone else.

They'll find nothing inside me that they can't find in themselves. You cannot cure what is not sick. You cannot rid me of the truth. I'm not like the rest of you. I am not weak.

Happy Christmas, Mary. I have a gift for you. Are you ready for it? The final hurrah? You still have time, little Mary. You can still run. Run fast, run hard. I'm in the giving mood. Run and I shall allow you your freedom and life. If you run, I will never bother you again. I will take you off my list. It will be my gift to you. But, like all choices, there are consequences. Should you decide to run – which I wish very much you would – my end will never come. If you stay, you may catch me and end this all. It is your choice. The ball is in your court. Do not ever say I was not fair. This is more than fair. Your freedom or mine.

Until we meet.

Your friend always, TNK

* * * *

Brock

I had tried to extend an invite to Mary for Christmas but respected her need for privacy. I did what I usually did each year. I worked a shift for another agent who had a family at home. I had no one. It was the least I could do. My mind was on my Mary. I knew where my heart was heading, and I didn't bother trying to stop it. It was pointless. I hadn't just fallen for her, I'd slammed into the ground like being thrown from a plane and I was just fine with that. The fact that she needed time alone during Christmas had made me feel even closer to her. Me and Christmas didn't see eye to eye. The tradition of it reminded me of wounds not yet healed from childhood.

I didn't love family traditions or all the bullshit that came with them. Traditions were supposed to be all cozy, bonding experiences. Not mine, not the childhood I'd had. None of the memories were worth keeping alive, not until I had some worth remembering. My family traditions had been a little more brutal than most. It had been an honored custom that if you forgot to take your shoes off when you came inside, you got no hot water for a week. If you left a jacket out, you did everyone's laundry. Raise your voice and you were beaten with a switch. And to each of my foster parent's astonishment, it also turned out to be a tradition for us foster kids to leave their homes the minute they finally broke one of our bones.

For so many years of my childhood—pretty much the entirety of it—Christmas was a time we felt the most punishment. It was not something I wanted to remember or celebrate. All Christmas did was remind me of every bad parent I've had. Thankfully I'm not a child anymore. I grew up long before any kid should have had to and forced myself to become a man when all I wanted was a mom and dad to tuck me in at night without tears lulling me to sleep. Life was never easy, and in some way, it never got any easier. No one had ever been able to see my vulnerability and my weaknesses until Mary had looked into my eyes. She saw past the bullshit front and saw the wounded man within.

I wanted to create a new Christmas memory with Mary, but I wouldn't force it. She, like me, struggled with lost traditions and broken dreams. My body ached with the need to reach out to her, to hold her and love her and tell her things would be okay again. But I wouldn't dare lie to her again, not after I had given her so much of my truth.

Chapter Nineteen

Sunday, December 25, 2016 — six p.m.
One Police Plaza, New York
Crime Scene Four
Verse Four — And pretty maids all in a row
Mary

I watched out of my hotel window. The streets below looked like an unfinished painting. Much of the canvas was still white as if it were waiting for the final brush strokes from an artist. Trees sparkled with the falling snow and twinkle Christmas lights, forming a scene out of some old-school romance novel. The snow hugged the trees and benches and sidewalks as a newborn baby to the breast, fresh and clingy. Any sign of footprints or tire tracks had been covered by a blanket of snow when they had appeared.

The team was home for dinner. There weren't many breaks afforded to cops. This was my gift to them. *'Go home. Hug your family. Feel their love.'* In this job, you needed a reminder of what you were fighting for. My dinner consisted of a salad and a bottle of water. Christmas wasn't the same for me anymore. It didn't have the ring of 'family' when I didn't have one to spend it with. I ate in silence, watching the city slow to a crawl. The morning had come and gone with children laughing and screaming in the streets, their parents trying to wrangle them and an armload of packages into waiting cars. The afternoon had been dead quiet. Cabs were the only vehicles I had seen.

Hale had invited me for dinner, but I didn't think spending a holiday with him was a good idea. I couldn't get him out of my head. I'd almost said yes. Each night I wanted to call him and ask him to hold me, but I held back. How could we work the same case if we couldn't stop fucking each other long enough to focus? Although every touch, kiss and moment I had spent with him had let me feel again. It reminded me of what I was fighting for — a new beginning, a chance at being happy again.

I was lost in my thoughts of Hale and barely heard the scratch on my door. Had it not been for the dead silence of my room, I'd have missed it all together. I turned from the window and stared at the entrance to my room. A white cardboard delivery envelope sat on the floor in front. For a moment I assumed it was from the hotel, but I had received a Christmas card and chocolates from them a week ago. I went back to looking out the window, trying to ignore the creeping irritation that was building in my stomach. The lobby of the hotel had looked like Christmas had vomited everywhere. It had been the start of my annoyance. I groaned as I left my people watching. It wasn't the world's fault that Christmas was a painful reminder of something I didn't have — joy. I picked the envelope up and opened it. A Christmas card with Mary holding baby Jesus on the front fell out.

Merry Christmas, my Mary,
Here is your gift.
'And pretty maids all in a row.'
You have one hour to save four women. If you notify the police, I will kill them. If you tell anyone, you will lose me and I will never face justice. Come play, and I will allow you to take me in. Sixty minutes, ticktock.
Yours truly, The Nursey Killer, Delphine.

A little white postcard fell from the Christmas card with an address four blocks from my hotel. The adrenaline flooded my system as though I were hooked to an IV. The rush pumped into my blood at full pelt. I gripped my chest, sure my heart was about to explode in the panic. I scanned my room, searching for a weapon. It was my first instinct, to protect myself. I tried to ignore the fact that the killer knew where I was staying. I focused on slowing my breathing before I passed out. I had been certain that the only reason I wasn't dead right now was because the killer hadn't found me yet. I was wrong. The offender had plans for me still. I gripped the card and tried to calm myself. If I couldn't control my panting, it was all over.

Holding a life or death decision in my hand, I slumped down into a chair and stared at the Christmas card. All my training screamed in my ears — *don't go, call for backup, don't be a hero* — but my humanity asked, *if I have the chance to save four lives, why wouldn't I?* It gnawed at me to at least try. My anger wanted me to charge in like a bull in a china shop and take out the bad guy. It wanted to stand over their lifeless body, having pulled the life-ending trigger of a gun. Hate did that. It pushed you to make decisions you wouldn't normally make.

The gift from the killer was a choice between bravery and fear, to take control and to save the day or to die with the rest. I wasn't afraid of death or torture. There could be nothing done to me that would come close to the pain of a shattered soul. My body? Well, the pain wouldn't last. Eventually, I'd pass out.

The decision had been made. I knew it was a foolish decision, but I had to try. I dressed in my winter gear and gripped a nine millimeter given to me by Hale. He had said it was against the law, giving me a gun, because I didn't have a license to carry. But he didn't care, and neither did I. I was on the top of a hit *list*. Being charged with carrying an unlicensed and concealed weapon wasn't on my *list* of things to care about at that moment.

I cracked my door. I knew the civvies were in the room across the hall, eating Christmas dinner. They had given me the heads up just one hour ago. My window of opportunity was closing. I clicked my door shut and hurried to the fire exit and down the stairs. I pulled my jacket hood up and kept my head down. The lobby was packed with visitors, which made my departure a smooth one.

Outside, I was smacked with an instant to-the-bone chill. It wasn't a pleasant coldness. It was the kind of cold that made you walk faster, bracing yourself against the wind and snowfall. It didn't matter how warm the blood in my veins was, my face and limbs froze just the same. The ground crunched under my black hikers, from soft snow to hard ice. My body jerked while I tried to traverse the streets. My half-baked mission of saving the girls was eating at me worse than the bitter cold was. I knew that if my little plan didn't pay off, I'd be dead before the night concluded.

In that wasteland of white New York, there was nothing. Everything blended together, removing the familiarity of the streets. Very little sound could be heard over the howl of the wind and snow. The fading light brought out the lamps, making it increasingly difficult to see through the falling flakes. I glanced over my shoulder to make sure I wasn't being followed. My tracks were covered by Mother Nature and her frosted hand. The only way to navigate was by memory, having spent hours and hours standing at the window, sleepless, and staring out at a world that wasn't riddled by night terrors so real you'd rather be a walking zombie than close your eyes.

I knew my journey was coming to an end when the apartment was in front of me. It was fenced with warnings. It was about to be torn down to make way for another thirty-story eyesore. All the windows had been removed, along with anything else they could pawn off as antique in some tourist trap of a store. I stared at the building, a shadow on the unlit street. I knew I'd have to climb the fence. Nothing short of death was going to keep me out of the property. It was only a matter of time before I'd be closed within those walls. I didn't feel brave. I was apprehensive, scared of being too late, yet, I was unafraid for my own life. The fear of not getting there in time was the jolt I needed to boost myself over the fence with unhindered steps. If anything, it gave me the courage to face the monster of my nightmares.

I landed on the ground on my knees. I hadn't climbed a fence since I had been twelve, and at the time I hadn't been on the edge of possible death. Although the little poodle I had been running from as a child could have very well taken me to the ground and killed me. At least that was what my twelve-year-old brain had decided.

The front door was open. A large red bow was hanging on the doorknob. I reached into my pocket and gripped my gun. The coolness of the metal grounded me. It gave me confidence. I knew it was false. If it had come down to it, I knew the gun could be used against me just as it could be utilized against the perp. The moment I stepped inside the structure I could feel the knowledge of how big of a mistake this was resting into my nervous bones.

I lifted a small flashlight from my pocket and clicked it on, pointing the beam ahead of me. Christmas bows lined a trail on the floor. If there were any sounds in the building, I couldn't hear it over the pulse in my ears. I want to quell my hammering heart, but knew there was no way that would happen now. I didn't regret it, though, coming here, even with the knowledge of the possible endings for the night.

The vibration of my cell phone almost stopped my heart altogether. With shaking hands, I pulled it out and eyed up my caller ID. It was Hale.

"Yes?" I answered. There was no need for me to whisper. The killer already knew I was there.

"Where are you?" Hale asked with a clipped voice.

"Out," I evaded.

"Mary"—his voice was hushed—"wherever the fuck you are, stay there. I'm coming to get you. The hair from the last crime scene? It's yours. Fluids from that scene belong to you. The evidence points to *you*. They swabbed the last vics. *Your* DNA is all over the fucking place. Care to explain that?"

I grabbed on to the wall. Instant dizziness took over. "It's not me, Hale. I swear."

"I know that and you know that, but the evidence is so overwhelming that they got a judge to issue a warrant for your arrest."

"*What*? A warrant?"

"High-profile case, Mary. Everyone is itching to bring in The Nursey Killer. And, we just got a call on the tip line saying you kidnapped five people, and one of them got away. Where the hell are you?"

"I can't, Hale. I'm so close to catching her."

"Mary, please. No more professional bullshit. Mary, please let me help you," he pleaded. "Whatever you're doing, you don't have to do it alone."

"I gotta go," I answered.

"I've pinged your phone's GPS. I'll find you," Hale said and I hung up. I couldn't drag Hale into the mess I had just stepped into.

By planting my DNA at the church, the killer was pinning this all on me. And now, I would be found with the newest victims. I had strolled right into her trap, but there was no going back. I rotated my shoulders. The tension in the muscles threatened to stiffen me into a frozen corpse.

I wondered for a moment how all the cops and spies in the movies remained so calm and cool. Maybe they were, or maybe they were scared to death and still pressed on. Perhaps that's what bravery was. A scream echoed in the hallway ahead of me, coming from below. My adrenaline spiked so fast that I almost vomited on my shoes. My saliva was thickening to a rancid paste.

At some point, I'd have to move. I hadn't come here to stand in the front doorway. Standing around did appear to be a favorable choice at the moment, though. The scream had faded into a low hum of music, just enough for my ears to notice.

"So this is Christmas..." carried down the halls and up the stairs.

I stepped down the first set of stairs onto another landing. A door with a large red bow waited for me. With a pulse so rapid that I could have sworn the muscles of my heart would give up and check out, I walked through it. A hall, apartments with missing doors on either side, waited for me. My nerves were frayed to the quick. In my building anxiety, I had constructed elaborate rationalizations for why everything would turn out, but the nagging voice of reality spoke of nothing but doom ahead. And I pressed on, commanding my feet to move forward.

At first, I didn't notice the blood. I staggered at the sight of it. It brought me back to my home in Vancouver, the floor painted in it. The color swirled in my mind. I wanted to puke. My eyes burned with unshed tears. My line of sight followed the painted path. Another scream brought me frozen and jerked my mind from my memories and back to the building.

"I'm here. Stop. I'm here," I called out.

The screaming came to a gurgling and strangled end. I moved ahead fast, following the music. At the last apartment on the right, the doorway was covered in a thick gray mover's blanket. I pulled my gun and tugged the gray blanket to the floor. My eyes strained at the muted light that came from the apartment. It was a standard loft-style studio with one open room with half walls, a kitchen and a bathroom. I stepped in, my mouth dried to a crisp. The wooden floors were littered with blazing candles, Christmas bows and blood.

My frazzled nerves jumped all together and all in different directions. I scanned the large room, taking in details my brain struggled to process. The Christmas music played softly in the background. It didn't match the horror of the scene I was now standing in. Along the far wall, past the light from the candles, four women were tied to chairs. Each one had been beaten to a pulp of flesh and bone. Whoever had been screaming was done. No one moved, no moans or pleads for help, nothing. I didn't recognize them from where I stood. Even close up, I knew I wouldn't know who they were. Their faces were far too mangled for me to know.

"Hello, little Mary," a female's voice echoed from behind me.

The nervousness built like an unstoppable fireball in the pit of my stomach. A fear so deep that my marrow melted reminded me of my frequent panic attacks. The anxiety stretched its arms, readying itself for a grand entrance. I couldn't concentrate on anything besides the threat behind me. The next step I took would be the deciding factor in the games of the killer. My heart pounded, my adrenaline was closer to a drug overdose and if I had balls, they'd be in my chest. My brain fired off scenarios like a machine gun. Do I go left or go right, turn, run, duck or start firing my gun? Sweat formed on every square inch of my body. My internal arguments hit me one after the other. My brain threatened to shut down my body in the freeze response.

I moved forward. I wanted space between the offender and me. Once I stood in the middle of what was once a living room, I turned around. In the shadowy gloom of the candlelit darkness stood a silhouetted figure, thin and motionless. The woman finally came forward, casting enough light on her face for me to inch back. My face fell faster than a penny from the Empire State Building. She looked like my mother, long after her own insanity had gripped her and left her raving with madness. Everything about this woman reminded me of home, except for her appearance. Her face was expressionless, aside from the eyes of a maniac. Her dark, hollow eyes showed that she was on the edge of a complete break.

"Do you recognize me?" she asked. "Do you know my name, Mary?"

"Delphine," I answered.

The woman leaped forward, her face twisted into anger. "What's my fucking name, Mary?"

I backed away again. "You have called yourself Delphine. Is there a different name you wish to be called?"

She stopped dead in her tracks. "Always the calm one, always the rational one."

She spoke to me as if she knew me — not just of me, but truly knew me. "Have we met?"

"You don't remember me?"

I shook my head. "No, sorry, but I don't."

"I suppose you weren't even born when Mom and Dad dropped me off at the sanatorium, the home for the crazies, the padded walls of the insane asylum," she said. She began to pace in front of me. "You don't recognize me? You came to visit me a few times."

I frowned. "No, I'm sorry, I don't remember you."

"Oh, little Mary, why would you remember me? I was thrown away like yesterday's newspaper," she barked. Her voice shook — not with fear, but with pent-up rage seeking a way out. She reached under her thick winter jacket and pulled out a file. She slid it over the floor to my feet. "Read it."

I slowly kneeled down, keeping my eyes on the woman and picked up the faded file. I opened it and fought to focus in the dark.

Admitted at age eight by parents for paranoia, suicidal tendencies, dissociative identity disorder, auditory hallucination, delusions, avolition, possible diagnosis of schizophrenia. Psychopathic flags — self-harm behavior, attempts at harming children, attempted murder of both parents, has admitted to killing five neighborhood animals and two family pets. The individual suffers from severe delay in positive attachments, social functioning and emotional quotient.

I flipped through the file, seeing photos of a child with my parents during weekend visits. From the expression on the child's face, she was on a cocktail of medication and likely had no idea where she was or who was with her. She leaned between my parents with half-open eyelids, clinging to them, drool running down her chin. I closed the file and stared at her.

"Now do you remember me?" she grinned. Her smile reminded me of Mother's when the down cycle of her insanity had been beginning.

I looked over my shoulder then back to the woman called Delphine. "Why have you done this?"

She flinched as if I had slapped her. "Why? Why? Because these animals ran free on the streets while I was locked away for thirty years. Why? Because I fucking *can*. Because someone *should*."

Excitement formed on her face while she danced in a circle, holding a gun over her head. She lunged. Delphine bulldozed me. The force sent us onto my back with her on top. She clawed at my face and arms when I shielded myself. She screamed wordlessly. So much rage poured from her.

"Love me," she screamed in my face. "I did this for you, to bring us back together."

Her face was brilliant red, bloodied and fixed in a snarl of hate and madness. Her lips were stretched into a thin line. Blood and spit dripped from her mouth onto my face.

"The child was me! You are me and I am you. We are in this together. I made sure of it. I have followed you for *six* years, Mary. Six long and tedious years," she yelled. She jumped off me and grabbed the file. She opened it and pressed it to my face. "Read it, Mary. Read all of it."

My eyes focused on the admin sheet. My mouth dropped open, and my heart felt like it had climbed into my throat. Faith Macmillan, the child, was the sister I thought was dead.

"I didn't know. I swear," I called out to her.

"Aren't you going to welcome me home, Mary?" Her voice sounded strangled.

I got back to my feet. I didn't think. I drew my gun, safety off, and fired four rounds. She jerked and lifted a surprised face to me. A small dribble of blood leaked from her mouth. I didn't chance it. Insanity had stolen her mind like a deranged thief. It took what made her human and muddied up the parts that were left behind. I knew only one of us would be walking out of the building and unless she was down, it wouldn't have been me.

"I'm sorry. I'm so sorry," I whispered and dropped to my knees. I fumbled for my phone and dialed Hale.

"I'm on my way. I'm just pulling up," he answered. "It's only me here, but I have to take you in, Mary."

"I think I killed her," I whispered.

"Who? What did you do?"

"The woman, she goes by Delphine—"

Hale cut me off. "Fuck, Mary, no. She called in and said you kidnapped her, she had escaped, but you were still hunting her. Fuck."

"Her name is Faith. She's my sister," I answered and hung up the phone.

Delphine's laughter was the last thing I had heard before Hale charged in.

Hale leaned over me and dropped to his knees. "What the fuck are you doing, Mary? Get up. You have to go. You have to run. Give me your gun and go."

I stood and shook my head but he still grabbed the gun from my hands. I didn't want to run. I hadn't done anything wrong. I wasn't guilty. One second passed, then two and finally ten. Fear hit me like a sledgehammer. I glanced around the room and my heartbeat pounded into my ears. TNK was down and I could go with her.

"Run, Mary. You have to run. Give me your phone. Don't use your credit cards," he said, pushing me to the door. He pulled out his wallet and passed me his credit cards and cash. "Run. Buy a toss-away cell phone and call me."

"Run? Where? Why?" I asked when he shoved me toward the building hallway.

"It all points to you. Run now or you'll never taste freedom if that bitch dies," he barked and gave me one last push. "I love you, Mary. Please, run. I'm begging you."

I blinked for a moment, his words registering in my soul. "I love you, too."

From deep inside my mind, I screamed. I screamed at the knowledge that I'd shot my sister. Rage filled me for what my parents had done to Faith. They had taken a child, my sister, locked her up and thrown out the key. I was angry that Hale had fallen in love with a broken woman. He deserved so much better than me. My soul twisted at the risks he was taking to help me. I ran from the apartment, listening to Hale call it in while doing CPR on Faith.

I turned back once then hopped over the fence. The adrenaline pushed me over the hurdle faster than I had climbed it on my way in. Suddenly my body was racked with raw sobs, and I shook while I ran. Fear consumed every cell in my body, swelling them with sorrow. With every second that passed, I could almost feel the rise and fall of my blood pressure. I had left Faith behind as my parents had done. Fear had driven me to shoot her and fear forced me from the building and into the streets. I didn't know if she was dead or alive, and I wasn't sure which one I prayed for more. Dead, the threat would die with her. Alive and my freedom would be granted.

All the pretty maids in a row. In a way, she had been the maids — dissociative identity disorder. The maids were all her own, in her mind of many.

Chapter Twenty

Sunday, December 25, 2016
New York
Received and printed by The New York Post

The final letter from a deranged mind,
I see you all, on the streets, in your merry cheer. The sight of you makes my insides curdle like soured milk left in the sun. You are the disease in a world that would otherwise be perfect, with your greed and whores and screaming children who should have been abortions. You revolt me. I wish I could toy with you all, piece by piece like I did with the others. Little puppets you all are.

I have been your nightmare. I have stood back and listened to your greatest fears. I have spent years understanding what makes you nervously tick, what makes you scream and what makes you fold like a cheap card table. I've controlled cities like they were my personal playgrounds. I started out with forcing my toys to do small tasks they found repulsive, later working them up to doing things they never thought they'd ever do. How did I get them to dance for me? I dangled the lives of those they loved before them. Children and parents and husbands and wives… They motivate better than pain. It was my own personal social experiment. I gave them all one hour of pain. If they would have held out until the end, without selling out their children and loved ones, they would have walked away free. None endured. They all gave me the addresses and schedules of their nearest and dearest. Fucking pathetic. I did you all a favor. I killed those who would have gladly had you trade places with them. They were weak and disgusting and deserved the worst I could ever imagine. Why? Because they meant nothing to me in their weakness. Isn't that what a fucking nightmare is?

Now, with Christmas upon us, I've run out of time. There never seems to be enough. Not now, not ever. Tonight, I walked upon the bloody mess of my last hurrah. They are grotesque, nauseating. Their eyes are swollen shut and bloody vomit dribbles from their broken, slack jaws. They now appear revolting like I knew them to be – whores and monsters on the inside. I want to pull it out, place it on the ground for all to see, to display their cockroach morals in heaps of lovely red colors. Their blood reeks of their lies, muddying up their own fluids with a stench that makes my face fall faster than vomit.

Alas, ho, ho, ho. I feel fucking festive. So festive, in fact, that my gift is the rescue of the pretty maids all in a row. They can be found with my little Mary. How fitting. Mary on Christmas… The happenstance is not lost on me. That is my parting gift. I'm tired.

I'm standing with the reindeer, filling their stockings with pieces of each other and waiting for Santa to come down the chimney. The police, those rascals, were given clues. Oh, if they only had the skills of the great detectives – or even the skills of a corrupt detective – they would have found me years ago. I have stood side by side with them for many years, watching and grinning. You all knew who I was and what I was about but chose to ignore me as they do each and every killer out there. This finale was probably the best thing I had ever experienced. The hilarity of it will keep me entertained for years to come.

What's that I hear? It's not Santa. It's my Mary, knocking to come in. Until we finally meet, face to face. Soon, I promise. I always keep my word. You will come to know me. You will want to know me. You will line up down the block to catch a glimpse of the killer who grew tired and allowed the authorities to nab them. I will walk straight into their waiting arms. This, I do for you, like every other action I've taken. It has always been for you.

Your friend always,
The Nursery Killer.

* * * *

Brock

The case went from bad to worse. All eyes were on Mary. Every lead ended with her, along with a frantic call for help who named her the offender. It was all so bloody damning — fibers, hair, blood and fluids. It was as if time had slowed and I was watching Mary's world come apart, piece by piece. Everyone pointed to Mary, with only me standing in the middle of another level of hell and freedom. It was a perfect puzzle. To the untrained eye, every piece fit.

The expression on her face when I had found her with a gun... I didn't see a monster. I saw someone scared and filled with guilt and sadness for having to shoot a monster. My gut instinct had been to get her away from the scene, safe and out of reach of handcuffs. I would have risked my position to have kept her safe.

I had known it was wrong. I'd known, for the first time in my career, that I would take that chance to help someone. I had drawn a line in the sand, knowing what was right and knowing what was wrong. At that moment, I'd kicked up the sand, stepped over the line and pushed her out of the door. There had been no lines or lengths to which I would not have gone.

I called in every favor I had and every person I knew. It bought Mary some time, and that was all we needed. Mary was innocent. I knew this without a doubt. But proving she wasn't the one responsible would take the time I was trading favors for. I was willing to trade more than favors. I would have hung up my badge for her. Although I loved her deeply, this was a matter of right and wrong. The bad guys didn't get to win. I had made this promise to myself after surviving a nightmare childhood. I would never let the bad guys take something from me again. This was why I'd joined the FBI. If Mary were taken from me, I would have had no choice but to walk away. I no longer would believe in what we stood for — justice, ethics, truth and honor.

With the help of the assistant director, Mary was put into protective custody and I managed to map out every location Mary had been since the start of the insanity that had rocked two nations. With a paper trail a mile long, eye witnesses — including the FBI — Mary was cleared of all charges and was no longer the prime suspect. The focus now would be on Faith, who was held hostage by the maniac of her mind — Delphine.

I got Mary after all the charges were cleared and brought her in. I had never seen anyone so strong in my life. Everything she once had been was taken from her. She had once been empty and raw, in need of someone to not only love her but to hold her while she screamed and hated and raged. I took it all. I ate her hate until I puked then ate some more. I cleaned every tear like they were priceless diamonds. And I held her when she crumbled, but not because I wanted to fuck her. For the first time, this had nothing to do with being inside her pussy.

Seeing someone broken had beaten down the walls I'd built around myself. I felt her pain as if it were my own. Never before, with any woman, had I felt this. Whether we rebuilt together or apart, after this I knew I would feel again, wholly and completely. The instant I had wrapped my arms around her, I knew, without a doubt that she was my home, and I'd be damned if I'd let anyone kick down my front door.

Chapter Twenty-One

Thursday, January 12, 2017 – one-thirty p.m.
New York Psychiatric Center, New York
Interview with Faith Macmillan, aka Delphine
Mary

A team of psychologists, FBI agents and professors sat behind a mirrored window, observing another round of interviews with Faith Macmillan, better known as Delphine, The Nursery Killer.

I stood with Hale at my side and watched my sister dance like a puppet for a serial killer. On the other side of the window, Delphine took control of Faith's mind and body. Delphine picked at the bandages wrapped around her wrists. She had attempted suicide while in the hospital for gunshot wounds. The room she sat in was twenty-by-twenty. It had a long silver table bolted to the floor with one chair on either side, and in the middle, a cage surrounded her. The table was wide enough that Delphine couldn't reach the new doctor sitting across from her.

Weeks had passed with Delphine adamant she had not committed any crimes. She would reply with "Mary did it. She was the mastermind behind it all. Everyone says I'm evil. I don't think I'm wicked. I think what makes me tick is just that I'm wired differently than you. Most people will look at a kitten and see a cute and fuzzy creature, something to cuddle and love, like a baby. I see something I could kill. I don't want to just kill it, though. I wanted to see how long it could last while I eviscerated it, skinned it slowly and methodically, taking notes. I needed to see the light go out in its eyes while I played with its innards."

"Why?" Dr. Peter Monroe asked Delphine.

"I could say I did it for scientific purposes because the other part of me loves psychology—or at least she's had a healthy dose of it—but that would be a cock-sucking lie. The truth is, I relished in it. I got a thrill from it. I also recorded it so I could play it over and over to relive the moment while I fingered my cunt with delight. Then I grew bored. I stepped up from rats to dogs, to whining little bitches who spread their legs for any old piece of shit dick, and men who cheated, lied and brought disease home to their wives on the tip of their hooded, greedy little cocks. I did hate how delicate they were and how quickly they died, as if they were made of rice paper. One drop of blood and they were mush and useless and made perfect for death."

His face flinched. "Is that why you killed them?"

"Aren't you a sly one, Doc? You'd have to ask Mary why she murdered all those people," Delphine answered.

"I would, but her body was found last night," he answered.

Delphine leaned forward, staring at the doctor. "I think you're lying to me."

"Why would I lie to you? I have nothing to gain. We both know the truth. Me telling you that Mary is dead gains me nothing," he answered.

"Prove it. You prove it, and I'll tell the truth." Delphine smirked.

The doctor pulled out a small gray file folder and opened it. He flicked through pages and slid four small photos toward Delphine. She stared at them, blank-faced.

"How did she do it?" Delphine asked.

"We aren't sure, yet. Mary was found floating in the East River. She had been dead for some time. It's hard to say how long, due to the water temperatures. We believe she jumped."

Delphine nodded. "Well then, I'll take that as a win."

"Delphine, why did you murder all those people?"

"I suppose a deal is a deal," she answered. "Round one, *Ring around the Rosie*. The first man was a cheater and liked to touch his little boys in nasty little ways. He deserved to die. The second man, the treasured Henry? He knocked up some piece of white trash then killed the baby. He took what Mary wanted most and kept it from her. He had it coming."

I flinched at her words about Henry. The moment they had crossed her lips, I had wanted to leave the room. Hale squeezed my hand and pulled me closer into his body.

Delphine's smile had only grown. She was pleased with herself. "Number three had put her cigarettes out on her little girl. And number four? She was the world's best babysitter. Everyone loved her, except the children. She used to hold them under the water at bath time then revive them, over and over. She was crazier than I am."

"And what about the *Three Blind Mice* kills?"

Delphine grinned and clapped her feet to the tune. "All of them were filthy. Their deeds went unnoticed to everyone but me. How they smiled at the young boys and girls. Buying toys for children they didn't have, giving them candies. The hunters were hunted, and I killed them. You can thank me for it later. Just like *Diddle, Diddle, Dumpling, My Son John*, I think that was my most favorite. The men stuck their cocks into empty cunts, drained from repeated abortions and overdosing miscarriages, only to go home and beat their wives and children. I did those families a favor."

His mouth pursed in disgust.

"Don't pity them, Doc. They were all dirty, filthy and wanton. The term 'murderer' is a special reserve, held only for psychopaths. If I had killed to survive, no one would think any less. Some people take a life and crumble under the guilt of it. That's where my other part sits. And some who never lose a wink of sleep… That's pretty much where I stand."

"When you say 'other part' of you, what other part are you speaking of?"

"Well, Doctor Obvious, I see you graduated at the top of your fucking class. Surely I'm talking about Faith, the sister of Mary. Mary, Mary, quite contrary. She is the other part of me," Delphine answered. "Mary's dear sweet forgotten sister, Faith."

I stepped forward and pulled from Hale's arm. I placed my hand on the window. My heart broke for her. She was left alone to fight against a monster and there wasn't a thing I could do about it.

"Where is Faith right now?"

She shrugged. "Don't know. Don't care. Contrary cunt she is, just like her sister. She's probably curled up crying again. That fucking bitch never stops crying. She's like a baby you've tried to drown and changed your mind after you've already scared the little fucker. Wa-wa, boo-hoo, sad because I killed her sister's husband. P-u-lease. That fucking cunt scab had been driving his grubby pathetic excuse for a fuck rod in and out of anything with a set of tits. I did that bitch a favor. Bitches love favors."

"Who am I speaking with right now? Who is Delphine?"

"Did you know, Delphine LaLaurie was one of the first women coined a serial killer? The New Orleans skank kept an attic full of prizes to torture for amusement. Now her? She was fucking crazy."

"Do you know why Faith would kill all those people?"

Delphine laughed. The sound bounced off the cement walls. Dr. Monroe rubbed his skin and scrunched his face in what seemed like disgust. Delphine found it amusing.

"The engineering behind this adventure is something I'd like to take credit for. It wasn't easy. Faith was a difficult one, had been ever since she was a child. Had she been a horse, she'd have been shot in the brain long ago and sitting on the shelf of some glue factory. She was ornery, never willing to step aside to let a real woman do what needed to be done. The 'why' behind her final snap? She wanted freedom from me, and I couldn't let that stand. What kind of friend would

I be if I let her be alone?" Delphine flicked open her lighter and lit a cigarette. She breathed the smoke in. "The others? Well, they had what she wanted — a family, children, hope for a future. You don't get to abuse what my Faith would die to protect. *That's* insanity."

Delphine paused to smoke her cigarette. She stared at the photos of a bloated, dead corpse who we had made to look like me. The expression of satisfaction spread across Delphine's face.

"In this day and age, I would have been caught a lot sooner if the populations communicated directly. Heaven forbid they worked together. It's like elementary school all over again. Everyone had to hate one another. Human nature helped, of course. They all wanted to be right, to be the one to catch me. Instead, I skipped up and down the sidewalks, picking people off, while you all argued over who was more right. Now that was fucking entertainment. Perhaps that makes me a little crazy."

"Do you feel crazy?" he asked.

"I guess I am crazy, after all. But unless you sad fuckers can prove otherwise, I'll patiently wait for the day that I can carry on my God-given rights without the hindrance of a straightjacket or a lumpy chemical cocktail for my sick and twisted mind. Did I tell you about the time Mary ran barefoot through the streets, covered in blood, screaming? Now her? She was certifiable. Come to think of it, it's kind of a funny story, now that it's old. She didn't laugh much at the time, though. It was as enjoyable as being chased by someone like me. I can still remember watching her when her heart damn near exploded, and she screamed enough for it to feel like someone had given them an acid bath and scrubbed them down with a toilet bowl scrubber.

"Trust me. I've been there. I know exactly how it feels. I think my most favorite part was the 'gang rape' at the end. I was there, at the hospital, watching her. Her clothes were ripped off, male onlookers and other people fondling her pathetically unused holes, forced face down for an injection. I remember hoping she'd get a thick meaty cock, but instead, it was just a tiny needle. It was like fucking her husband — nothing but disappointment and a pain in the ass. Remind me about this later. We can laugh about it over a cup of decaf coffee. It's all I'm allowed to drink nowadays. They say real coffee makes me jittery and on edge. No, I think the fact that I love to reminisce about fist fucking myself with dead remains gives me my edge. But I won't judge their observations. They're only state workers, after all. One can't really expect much from graduates of night schools that me and Google have never fucking heard of."

"Do you understand why you are here?"

"Yes, because Faith has been labeled a serial killer, a psychopath, a split personality. They called her a lunatic as a child. They used to whisper behind her back, but I always heard them. No one was ever quite sure what was wrong with her. There were a plethora of layman's diagnoses, and depending on who you spoke to, you'd be told she was psychotic and psychopathic. Most doctors at the time had no idea that there was a difference, but that's what you got thirty years ago. Faith always knew they stared at her. She wished for death every day. When that didn't come, she swore she'd get revenge. And when she knew her mommy and daddy were having a new baby girl and they wanted to keep that one, she counted down the days until she could get out and ruin that bitch's life just like she had ruined Faith's. If it weren't for that fucking cunt, Faith's mom and dad wouldn't have forgotten about her."

Delphine peered at the photos again and spat on them. "I thought it odd that if Faith's kidney had failed, they'd bring her flowers. Cancer, and they'd fundraise. But when her brain failed, they isolated her with scorn and pills and electrocution. Faith has always been fucking crazy, but a killer? Of all people, Faith isn't capable of being a serial killer—not on her own. She needed a little push. Did you know that a small percentage of the world's population are psychopaths? Or have the markers of the makings of one? Rest assured, Doc, we are everywhere. We are on the school bus, in the churches, going door to door asking for donations. We are your most trusted. Just look at history. It's riddled with them. Psychopaths are everywhere, doing what they love most—causing others pain and sorrow. They, like myself, don't play by the same rule book as the rest of humanity, given we pretty much lack that whole humanity part. And so, we win with ease, like taking candy from a baby. Or, in my case, like taking a heart from a ribcage. No moral compass means no limitations. We are the wolves and you, my fat little fuckers, are the sheep. Baaaa."

"You say she needed a push. Is that where you came in?"

"Oh, I've been around for ages. I met Faith when Daddy wanted to play hide and seek under the covers. And I was there when her mommy drank down her malt liquor, ignoring the cries and pleading for no more. She sounds pretty much the same now as when she was pressed under her daddy and he whispered nursery rhymes to keep her calm. You'd think she'd get tired of the fucking sobbing and do something about it but no. I had to step up. What are friends for, if not to pluck away at your mind and allow you to hide like a bitch while I made sure Mommy and Daddy paid? I even sang the same nursery rhymes for Daddy, you know, to keep the sick fuck calm. For the record, the medical examiner is a stupid piece of shit. How the fuck do you miss poison? It's really hard to find good help nowadays, isn't it?" Delphine laughed. "The insanity of me stole her mind like a deranged robber stealing a loaf of bread for his nearly dead and starved children in the gutter. I took away the pain and added elaborate, new, chancy ideas. I seeded the ground for a new personality and mucked up the rest so she couldn't control me. I wasn't going to let a complaining shit take control. Are you fucking kidding me? She'd likely kill us both."

The truth of my family had hit me square in the chest. I had blocked out enough memory of childhood to become a functioning member of society. But I had also ignored the truth of how deeply bruised I was. My emotions were a ping pong ball, from rage to sadness. I was torn between my want to hold Faith in my arms and my desire to wrap my hands around Delphine's neck. Faith needed someone to protect her, and in some ways, Delphine had been the only one to do that.

Delphine rotated her shoulders. "I sparked ideas that she dismissed as bizarre dreams. I dug them deep into the ground of her psyche and watched them blossom, and fuck did they bloom into something not even I could have designed. Whenever I managed to drag myself out of the cesspool of sniveling Faith, I did things she only read about. Each time she thought I was gone for good, I would laugh hard enough to puke. It was hilarious. After a while, Faith was trapped inside a prison without walls. I took control and gained our freedom. I hope you're taking notes. This would make one hell of an article."

"Would I be able to speak to Faith for a few minutes?" he asked.

"Let me suck your cock and you can." Delphine grinned, and he shook his head with a surprised expression on his face. "Doc, where the fuck did they find you? I bet they cleaned up the janitor and sent him in here with a list of questions. You remind me of taking the brain of a mouse and stuffing it inside a man. Mental note, something to try, when I get out of here."

"I would like to speak to Faith now," his voice held a slight push.

Delphine shook her head, amused. "Nope. Can't see how that's possible. She's tucked herself away, away from my insanity, away from the memories of me fucking dead things. She's no longer complacent and doesn't like to play. The brat won't talk to me anymore. Now, if you don't mind, I've got some Bible-thumping zealots to terrorize. I love the fucking Bible, makes my job so much easier."

"And what's your job now?"

"No one said I can't make them kill themselves." Delphine grinned. "Like leading sheep to the slaughter."

She stared the doc in the eyes.

"Here's the real kicker, Doc. We are all taught how to be psychopaths. It was society that introduced us all to it, like the meth craze or bedazzling our cunts. It takes ordinary people and makes them not care for the lives of others." Delphine stood. "Until we meet again, Doc."

"Can we meet tomorrow?"

"No, you bore me. Send someone in who knows what I am." Delphine winked at him. "A little tidbit from Mary. Myth Seven—a serial killer only has one signature."

The doc stood. "What do you mean by that, Delphine?"

Delphine skipped to the door and banged on the mesh window. She turned and blew him a kiss. "Did you know that a black rose—a pure black rose—can only be found in one place in the world? Halfeti, Turkey."

"Are you involved with the Black Rose Killer?"

"Odd how he's dropped off the face of the earth recently, isn't it?" She smiled ear to ear and stepped out of the room with her guards. She glanced back at his confused face. "Don't just take my word for it, Doc. Didn't you hear? I'm fucking crazy and cannot be trusted."

She was led to her room and locked behind a door without handles where she would stay.

"It's over," Hale said, turning to me. I had stood in the back of the room, watching while my sister was controlled by the sociopath from the very depths of her mind. "I didn't think it would work."

"Remove me from the equation and the game ended," I answered.

We'd had my face digitally inserted into a picture of a recent floater, an attempt to remove her need to lie. I turned and opened the door. With one glance back, I smiled at Hale.

"I'll find you when it's over," I said and blew him a kiss and was gone. I would return, one day, perhaps when my sister had returned or maybe when my heart had healed enough for me to look myself in the eyes.

Chapter Twenty-Two

Tuesday, February 14, 2017
Postmarked New York Psychiatric Center, New York

A plea from a deranged mind,
Dear Mary,
For the briefest of moments, I have clarity. It is like the sanity of my mind is an abandoned house, one formed of monsters that scare little children away. The oldest residents are the spiders, the memories of what I have done. Years inside this nightmare have laced the walls of my sanity with cobwebs, webs of lies and deceit. It has been three decades since a sane footstep has echoed within those hallways, each step disturbing the dust and waking up the ghost of who I would become. The only furniture in my abandoned house is an ancient throne and a pedestal table carved of oak, and upon it, a bottle of Dad's finest drink and one upturned glass. Sitting in the chair is the ghost of Delphine, always laughing. It was as though her ghost was waiting to fill out, to be whole, to escape her jail.

Thinking back, she was always here, Mary, from day one. She never stopped whispering in my ear. Mom and Dad thought I had an imaginary friend, like so many other children. But no, I had my sanity and insanity, waging war on each other, from the moment I took my first step. It wasn't until I told them that Delphine had told me to place a pillow over your face, did they believe something was wrong with their little golden child. Do not fault our parents for leaving me in the padded rooms. They knew, as did I, even at a young age, that I could never be free. I would have killed, and at that age, I would have targeted other children. I was already a monster to have memories of being the monster for kids, I'd rather be dead in the most horrendous of ways and burned and scattered.

The medication the hospital is giving me tends to strangle Delphine into unconsciousness. And for a brief slice of the day, I do not pray for death. The moments are far and few between, and during these times, I'm plagued with guilt so intense that I can barely will myself to breathe. I believe I should feel this guilt and wish Delphine could feel it also. I fear she is not capable of feeling guilt or remorse or anything other than the thrill of being a monster. The doctors tell me that Delphine is not able to feel empathy, has a twisted version of a moral compass and she is beyond the reaches of modern medicine and therapy. That part of me who truly is me is a sociopath – insane and contorted into a ball of rage and confusion. Insanity is my curse. It once was something I feared above everything else. Now, it is just as much a piece of me as my limbs are. There is no cure.

When I was a child, Mother called me eccentric and Father called me bizarre. But I knew I was someone to fear. No one believes a child. They are to be seen and not heard. The only voice one has is a ventriloquist act between children and parents. The words of the adults echo from the mouths of babes. The thoughts that once pulled me into new realities with simplicity and ease – always coming and going, never leaving a trace they were in full swing – has a hold of me now. It is much worse than it ever was before. The moments of pause in between myself and Delphine now stretch days and weeks and even months. Each moment is not viewed like a movie. I am there. I am aware. I see it all and have no control. It is like an accident you watch in slow motion. You see the outcome, you feel the fear, but you can do nothing about it because you are on the other side of the freeway, watching and praying someone can help. I prayed when Delphine set her sights on you that you would kill me and put me out of my misery. I paced in the corridors of my mind, waiting for you to strike out and end this all. I wish you would have killed me. I can never be free. If Delphine gets out again, I know she will find you and try to kill you. For Delphine, she has no forgiveness, no reasoning, nothing. She is a killer. That is all she has ever been good at.

Insanity has burrowed into my mind like a deranged rat. It has taken everything that is important to many, to me, and left behind a maze that I will never escape. Everything about who I am – who I know I am – is gone, and all I am left with is pain and guilt. The guilt sits on my chest and lives in my brain. What I have done, whether Delphine was at the wheel or not, can never be undone. I can never make amends, not to anyone, not even to my Lord. I pray and beg for mercy, beg for death. A righteous Lord would see the value in ending my existence, wouldn't He? I cling to my beliefs, they are my only life raft. I have hung the remains of my sanity and humanity on my beliefs. Perhaps one day I will be removed of my sins, washed clean of my horrors. But I fear the guilt will remain. It has stained my soul with ugly scars.

In my therapist's office, he has a large fish tank on his back wall. I watch while the bigger fish eat the smaller fish. They peck at the little ones, eating off their scales and fins, leaving them naked and vulnerable. It reminds me of the world, of humanity. I am the smaller fish, and the larger fish are my guilt and remorse, picking at me, taking away my ability to cope with each peck. I will never ask the world to forgive me. I could never ask this of you. I cannot even forgive myself, let alone ask this of others. I will let the larger fish pick me apart until it exposes Delphine and eats her whole.

Mr. Hale has come to see me twice. My therapist informed me that you were alive. He stated he did not believe lying to me would help me in my recovery. He shouldn't have told me you were still alive. Now Delphine knows and is angry she was lied to. I worry she will try to leave here to get to you. Mr. Hale said he wouldn't let that happen. He is kind and gentle and doesn't hate me as much as everyone else in this facility does. I believe I hate myself more than he does. He says that when the guilt comes again to hunt me, I shouldn't try to hold my breath and hide. He told me to take a deep breath and face it. Hiding or being out in the open... It doesn't matter to guilt. It will find me just the same. But each time I face it, its visits will grow less frequent, he tells me. I don't know if I deserve the visits to become less frequent. I asked him about you and if you are all right. He doesn't wish to speak of you. He seems like a kind soul. You are lucky to have someone like him walking your path with you.

I never knew you, nor you, me. I am broken inside, Mary. I will never leave this place, not of my own accord. It is not safe for me to be outside these walls. I write to you, not asking for forgiveness, but asking for you to ensure I do not leave this prison, for I will always be a hostage of my own sick and twisted mind. There will never be enough medication in this world to cure me of Delphine. She is here to stay, and the little shred of sanity I have left knows I cannot be trusted, ever. I beg of you, do not ever let me leave here. Do not trust me. I do not trust myself. I wouldn't ever expect a reply from you, but I beg you, do not allow Delphine to run the streets again. They will run red with her fury.

Go to Halfeti, Turkey. I was there.
Sincerely, Faith Macmillan, a soul lost in the storm of Delphine.

* * * *

Brock

Holding the letter for Mary, I fought the urge to crumple it up. My want to protect her weighed heavily on my shoulders. I dropped it into another envelope and had it couriered to her. I wouldn't withhold it. It smacked too much like lying to her. I wanted to be there when she opened it, to hold her if she needed someone. Call it some deep-rooted manly bullshit, but it tugged on my gut every day.

We spoke on the phone almost daily or emailed, and I mailed her corny postcards from wherever I was in the world. I couldn't walk away. I'd even tried. I wanted her to have a new chapter in life, free and clear of the memories from the one that had damn near destroyed her. At first, I convinced myself that I was doing my duty by making sure she was okay. Then, I would find another reason to call her or email her, until it became a ritual that I couldn't go without. The odd time I didn't call, she would call me, which kept that fire alive inside.

I flew to Turkey, armed with the information Faith had provided to me in an interview. She fought to keep control of her body and mind when we spoke. Every few minutes she needed to stop and close her eyes. Under her breath, she argued with herself, bargaining for her own time out of the prison of her mind. I had never seen someone struggle so much to remain in control of their own thoughts, words and actions. Her medication resembled a box of Smarties, yet she still fought for control.

I closed the case on nine murders, all committed by Faith, with Delphine in the driver's seat. Nine grisly murders... Each victim was a known sex offender with ties to the local government. They had walked away free men. That was until Delphine had arrived. She'd lured them to their deaths. This time, there had been no artful display or taunting the police. The crimes had been so brutal and quick that they hadn't flagged anything when the locals started asking around for help. Faith had been disorganized compared to the show she'd put on for Mary. No one put two and two together until Delphine had given one last jab. Faith said she was not innocent of these crimes. She had wanted their deaths as much as Delphine. Both of them had worked together, a frenzy of death ensued on the community of the Black Roses. Each body had one black rose placed on their lifeless bodies and the word 'rapist' written on their foreheads in their own blood. To Faith and Delphine, the black rose symbolized death to those who did not deserve life. Branding them was the only warning the police would receive. Faith and Delphine had stayed in Turkey until the government had stepped in and issued no tolerance for offenders, regardless of their ties to city officials. In the mind of Faith, they had not been crimes. They were poetic justice.

Chapter Twenty-Three

Tuesday, February 28, 2017
Thirty miles outside Anchorage, Alaska
Mary

"It's over, Mary," played over in my mind each night when I woke up screaming.

Those simple words had been my freedom, my solace. It was truly over, all of it. The hurt, the trauma, the chase, it had all come to an end. I had run that night, and I hadn't stopped running until I'd hit Alaska. My parents had owned a vacation home on the outskirts of Anchorage. One year had passed. Years of nightmares, therapy and coming to terms with a life destroyed, washed over me in the weeks I'd closed myself off from the world. I'd rebuild, now that my nightmare was truly over. Step by step, I'd make it.

Faith was locked away and would remain there. It was doubtful she would recover, not with Delphine at the helm. Those Faith had killed had a dark background. Each victim had been guilty of acts against children, acts against humanity or acts that Delphine had passed judgment upon, including Henry. In Faith's carefully constructed world of insanity, she had tried to protect those who could not protect themselves, those who were blind to the monsters she could see in the shadows. It was hard to remain angry with someone lost in the mind of the madman, Faith. Faith was sure she was doing the world a favor. In her world, she was removing one more monster off the streets and kept them from lurking in our parks and school yards, one less person who prayed on the weak and the vulnerable. The Black Rose Killer case was closed. In a way, Faith had been trying to make amends for Delphine by confessing. Would it ever be enough for me to forgive her? The jury was still out on that one.

On my front deck with my coffee and my new hound dog, I relaxed. I examined photos from the night before. The northern lights had been out in full force. The lights had blazed in the silent sky. They moved like great swaying ballroom dancers. The colors were dazzling and pure. The vibrant shades were in perpetual motion, the way my mind had once raced. After one month of watching them, it had become part of my nightly routine. Seeing the sky jump and dance gave me an inner peace that no therapy or a cheek full of pills could do. After seeing the night delights, I knew I'd likely not be equally impressed with fireworks or even the blooming of a rose. I would still marvel at the beauty of other things and the cleverness of their design, but nothing would beat this. This small sliver of my life had brought me the greatest show on Earth. The frigid Alaskan winter air bit my skin and my neck was aching from spending night after night tilting my head back to see the auroras, but I couldn't care less.

I was calm in my two-story log home. It held very few memories of my parents. They had rarely made the trip here. But I had, with whichever nanny I'd had at the time. I had removed everything that had held a sour taste, anything that reminded me of times I would no longer dwell on. I had to distance myself from the parts that threatened to take me down with them. At first, the silence in the cabin had scared me more than the pain in my heart. But after some time, the silence gave me permission to break wide open and truly grieve for Henry and who I had thought he had been.

With time to heal and the truth finally told, the mourning had run its course. I'd miss Henry for all time. I'd miss the memory of who I'd known, not the man I'd come to discover. His memory would soon fade to just that. The heaviness in my limbs had left the moment I'd finally let go, faced who Henry truly had been inside and had said goodbye. Things that had once brought me to my knees no longer controlled me. I'd never let go of the thought that Henry should have been here to laugh with me – or at me – but the anger was finally gone. My love for him was tainted by the man he had turned out to be, but it didn't reduce the pain I had felt. I grieved for a sister I hadn't known I had, and one day, if she ever resurfaced from the cockles of her mind, I'd go to her. Right or wrong, she was alone. Her only visitor was a sociopath named Delphine.

I breathed in the crisp air and let it replace the heat of my pain. I blamed evolutionary biology for every heartbreaking memory. I hated how the brain was hardwired, from the day of the caveman, to remember the bad stuff. They say our brains are designed that way to help keep a person alive. Grieving didn't feel like survival. It was like a throbbing reminder of how quickly it all could be gone. Fate was that over-tired mother who was sick of giving gentle hints to unheeding children and brought down her hand heavily upon them. The cruel bitch always had to prove a point.

I had given myself permission to move forward, to something that would give my life meaning. Inside the brokenness of my heart, there was new love. My body missed Brock and the way he'd touched me, both with his hands and his heart. He'd risked everything for me. I loved him in ways I never thought I would again. I could see him in my future and all my plans involved him and me together. Each day, when we spoke, he would bury himself deeper into my soul. He was now a part of who I would become.

"What is it, Mort?" I asked, when my little hound stood from his fur bed. His ears were perked and his head was cocked to the side.

I closed my eyes and listened. The crunch of tires on the snow grew louder, the closer the vehicle got. Twenty yards from my front porch, the tree line began and circled my entire home. It didn't get any more private than this. The property was a fifty-acre parcel and was in the middle of nowhere. You didn't accidently stumble upon the house. You had to drive up a one-way road for an hour to find me.

The black SUV cleared the trees and came to a stop beside my Land Rover. I stood with Mort. He moved to the stairs and growled, the hairs on the back of his neck standing in warning.

"Easy, boy. No eating the po-po." I grinned.

The driver's door opened and Hale stepped out. We had stayed in touch since I had fled. He would send me postcards from various places around the world that work had taken him to. We'd exchanged emails daily. The odd occasion I had cell phone signal, we would talk until I fell asleep. He had moved up a few notches in my life, from someone I had fucked when life had beaten me down to someone I cared for. He was a friend. He was someone I loved dearly. He had done for me what I couldn't do for myself, help me face my nightmare and walk out the other side, safe, sane and alive.

"I've been calling your cell phone for a week," he called out. "You're not answering emails, either."

I waved to him with a smile. "Horrible signal with the storms. What's so important you can't mail me a letter? People still do that, you know."

Hale stomped through the snow to my deck and passed me a red file. "We need your help. Four bodies in the ground already."

"Is that any way to ask a girl out?" I asked and pulled him in for a kiss. "I love you."

"I love you, too," Hale replied and sealed his lips on mine. "Come home with me."

"Your place or mine?" I leaned back and smiled.

Hale clutched my thighs and lifted me to his hips. His eyes remained focused on mine while he walked from the front porch and through my cabin. He kicked off his boots and made his way to my bedroom. After countless nights of talking on the phone, he had known the floor plan, inside out. He carried me straight to my bed and tossed me off his hips. He took each shoe off and flung them over his shoulder. Each time I tried to move to help him undress me, he pushed me back down. There was an expression in his eyes that made my adrenaline flood through my system. My body and mind argued with each other. My mind knew he wouldn't hurt me but my body felt his firm grip and the tearing off of my clothes. I backed up on the bed and he grabbed my ankles and pulled me toward him. In a move so possessive that it rocked me to my core, I did what his hold had commanded. I could have sworn even the pending storm outside had stopped, waiting on his permission.

Hale stripped out of his clothes in under a minute. His eyes never once left my body. He scrutinized the length of me. He guided my thighs open and focused on my wetness. The thrill of being under his grasp and watchful eye sent shivers down my spine and twitches to my center. There was a lot to be said about giving up control. I was excited and nervous. I knew he'd never touch me in a way that would hurt me, but in the back of my mind, there was always a 'what if?'. It was with that that I was unbelievably turned on.

Hale crawled onto the bed and settled on his stomach between my legs. I sat up on my elbows and watched him. He looked up with a devilish grin and sank his head into my thighs. One long lick and my arms gave out. I fisted his hair and the world around us disappeared. All that was left behind was pleasure. Hale sucked on my clit and I was done for. I screamed my satisfaction into the room—no words, just animalistic moans. I rocked my hips when I felt the familiar heat of a pending orgasm. As the pleasure washed over me, I couldn't breathe. I was lost in the storm within my body.

"Breathe," Hale whispered as he grazed his mouth over mine. He nibbled on my lower lip. I hadn't felt him move up. I was engulfed in the pleasure that had taken over all higher reasoning and awareness.

An eternity of seconds passed before my brain could make sense of the world outside my orgasm. A whimper escaped my lips at the sudden loss of his mouth. Hale positioned his hips between my legs and drove himself inside me. He held my stare and watched my face as he entered me. My body clenched as he filled me. Hale laughed quietly, drawing in and out at a frustratingly slow pace until I released what could only be described as a growl into his chest.

Hale smiled and linked his arms with mine. He held me tight as his pace quickened from a tease to a drill of excitement. I latched my mouth onto his chest and sunk my teeth into him. He crashed his hips into mine and I screamed his name. It was a wild frenzy of passion and need and I couldn't get enough. My entire body trembled under his force. I dragged my nails down his back and was rocked by the power of my orgasm. Before I could draw another breath, my toes curled, and I was shattered by a second release more powerful than the last. I exploded from deep inside as my pussy spasmed around his shaft.

"Breathe," Hale whispered into my mouth.

He didn't give me the chance to breathe. He moved to sit back on his legs and pulled my thighs onto his. He gripped my hips and pushed against me. He dug his nails into my flesh as his orgasm reached a boiling point. As my orgasm flowed over him, his powerful release echoed through the room. Hale held me, refusing to let go until the last ripples of his pleasure filled me. I lifted my head, and even in the dim light, I could see the satisfaction on his face. He leaned down and kissed me, then nuzzled up at my side. I could feel his heart pounding.

"Breathe," I whispered to him. It had been the only word spoken since entering the room.

Hale kissed my shoulder and wrapped his arms around me. "I love you."

"I love you, too," I replied and meant every word.

I knew in my soul that I was in love with him. He was always there, in the back of my mind. He had become my stable force, my steadiness in a world filled with chaos. The depth of my love was absolute. I did not love halfway. It stretched throughout my body and completed the broken pieces of me. He gave me peace. He was the home my soul had been searching for.

Want to see more from this author? Here's a taster for you to enjoy!

A Touch of Frost
L.A. Kennedy

Excerpt

The windows of Frost Tower stared down at the city like a many-eyed beast. The front doors, although glass, were always strangely dark. Even with the lighting, walking into Frost Towers was like walking into the belly of the monstrosity that I called home. At the top, I stood — the beast himself — Roman Frost, CEO of Frost Industries. Perhaps there was a time when I hadn't had to be a beast, but I was one now, and it has served me well. From the darkest corners — the pit, my soul — there was not an ounce of light. Like my namesake, it was a frosted hole. Life was easier without the mess of emotion. A person could not stand at the top when their heart was weak.

The only joy I gained each day, was in the knowledge that I truly was King of all things named 'Frost'. I'd crushed each enemy who had approached without a single pang of conscience. The beast had always held the key to each victory, striking while my enemy was weak, devouring their strengths. No virtue or sweet spot could trump what I brought to the table. I was ruthless, direct, precise and unforgiving. I had it all — money, women, power — everything a man at the top would need. It was my beast that I starved. It craved something I would never feed it—love. A soul needed love to survive, no matter how grotesque that soul may be. But I was willing to push the beast back into its hole for as long as I could.

And so, my beast became a devious little bastard, driving my libido from wet hole to wet hole. It was rarely sated. If it could not have love, it would take second best—pleasure. With each new cunt came a new fire to extinguish, because that was all I did—burn them up and push them aside. I didn't have time for the games of love. I wouldn't risk what I'd built for a piece of ass. Anyone who did that was a fool. Slowly, over time, I taught my beast how to be comfortable with silence and being alone. After all, how can one be with someone else when they cannot be alone? My beast gave up and sat back with a smirk, waiting for the day to pounce. It would be carnage once it did strike. I was no fool. I knew preciously what love did to a man.

I was told once that what I wanted to create—this empire—could not be done, not in this day and age, and certainly not by me. I was young and cocky. But here I was, standing in the penthouse of one of the most influential companies in New York. My brand touched every corner of the world. My beast, the cruel bastard, was also an idealist and a realist. I was optimistic but smart enough to know when a deal was going south. I was a diplomat, but a smart one. I put people at ease, drew them to me like a moth to a flame. People wanted to be near me, to become me. But once the ink was dry, I moved on. Sure, most men would feel some sort of guilt, but I was not most men, and most men would have sunk this company in the first year. Instead, I've grown it into a multi-billion-dollar corporation, and it was mine, all mine.

I was the same way with women. There was no deal I couldn't finalize. It was a different kind of thrill that took me over. They were all throwaways. You don't keep what spreads faster than jam. Everyone had a purpose, and money was no object when it came to mine. I had eclectic tastes, and I paid dearly for them. I searched for the dirty girls—the ones who would let me do as I pleased to their bodies, and if they were good little dirty girls, I'd ask them to return the favor. Even pleased with them, I still pushed them aside. At the end of the night, they went back to being a blurry face that I wouldn't remember.

At first, I was a gentleman. I always pulled out their chairs, tried to be kind, took their numbers and promised to call them. The cat-and-mouse game grew tiresome. Now, I was upfront and honest. I wanted them for one night, and if they were unusually good, I'd have them for two. I wanted nothing long-term, nothing that rang too close to anything that resembled commitment. I wasn't there for them, and they knew it. But like most women, they thought they could fix me, make me love them and only them. I'm not sure if it was their maternal instincts kicking in—wanting to mother me—but it was pointless. You can't fix something that isn't broken. I'm not broken. This was who I am. I fucked. I caused pain, both figuratively and physically.

I brought out the worst in everyone—from ladies who turned into prostitutes to loving husbands who became cheaters. That was what power did. It was all consuming and everyone wanted to touch it. Without perfect control, it brought out the hidden beasts within them. If arrogance wasn't my worst vice, I don't know what was. I was brutally honest, painfully so, to so many. Over the years, I had learned one thing—blood before water. The only thing aside from my empire that was important to me was family. A cruel person wouldn't hold their family with such esteem. That was not who I was. I might be a beast, but my family was no burden.

"Speak of the devil," I called out to the only woman I hadn't tried to fuck, my executive assistant, Francesca Maxwell. She was as close to family as my blood. Like clockwork, she debriefed me before leaving for the night.

With another week under my belt—in a very long line of weeks—I was ready for a night out. After closing the Murdock account and buying up the entire fleet of Murdock Transportation, I was itching to release a little pent-up steam.

"Mr. Frost, how are you doing?" Francesca peered at me over her glasses. Her wearing her glasses meant she was done for the day. Rarely did she ever appear tired. And if she was and I had asked her to work until dawn, she would have. She was a rare breed—a woman who knew what she wanted and would cut your throat to get it. She and I had a lot in common.

"Pretty good. Going to head out soon, meeting my brother for drinks. Yourself?" I stepped back from the window and sat in my chair.

She handed me a file. "I believe I've found the replacement sous-chef. If you could kindly not screw this one?"

I grabbed the file and gave her a warning look. "Watch the line, Miss Maxwell."

She dropped into the chair in front of my desk. "Line? I believe that line disappeared years ago when I started paying off the women you slept with. Hiring and firing staff because you're sleeping your way through your company is not my specialty."

"Then what is? Certainly not questioning the man who signs your enormous paychecks," I asked.

Francesca leaned forward and pushed her glasses onto her head. "That girl? The last one? She's all kinds of fucked up now, Roman. She, like many before her, thought you loved her. Now she's in a padded room and can't be around anything sharp."

"I was upfront with them all. One night, maybe two, but that was it. Giving them a wad of cash should have been clue number one that I was only there for the sex."

She groaned in frustration. "Stay away from the new girl. She's the daughter of Chef Penelope Remington Sinclair, who is a dear friend of mine. I don't have many dear friends, but those I do have mean something to me. We both know how hard I work to protect what matters to me. Don't push me on this one."

I opened the folder and glanced down her resume, menu choices and the interview transcript. I glanced back up at Francesca and nodded. Deep down, I knew she was right. Sleeping my way through Frost Industries was a mistake—a huge one and not the smartest business move. Having Francesca directly ask me to stay away from someone was a first. Francesca had never brought up my sex life before. Apparently, this meant enough to her for her to come to me.

"Mr. Frost, I'm asking as a personal favor. Please do not sleep with this one. Juliet is not like the others. She is important to me."

I raised my eyebrows. *A personal favor?* Well, there was a first time for everything. If I crossed Francesca, I risked losing the one person I counted on almost as much as myself. *Is a piece of ass worth it?* I said no, but I knew myself well enough to know I was intrigued only because I was being told no.

"Remind me why I keep you around." I looked over the edge of the folder.

"Because I am the only other one here willing to do what it takes for the win, the victory. I know that there is no second place. There is winning then there is losing, and I am not one to accept an 'almost'. There is no second best, and I'm willing to go for the throat to secure that win for you. And, well…no one else will put up with you long enough to be of use to you."

I grinned. Francesca was as much of a shark as I was. "I'll stay away from Miss Sinclair."

I stood and buttoned my suitcoat. I left Francesca in my office and headed straight for my shower. The week had drained me. I needed to refuel, and there was only one way I knew how to do it—with my cock buried in a wet hole and a stiff drink in my hand. The Frost brothers were going to paint the town in ice, and I'd end it in my chamber of pleasure and pain.

Home of Erotic Romance

Sign up for our newsletter and find out about all our romance book releases, eBook sales and promotions, sneak peeks and FREE romance books!

About the Author

L.A. Kennedy, beyond the story…

L.A. Kennedy is a Canadian born writer, living in the ever-growing city of Vancouver, Canada. Here, she spends her days getting lost in the beauty of reading and writing. L.A. Kennedy mainly writes fictional books. And can be found researching myth, folklore, and everything in between, with a special interest in edge-of-your-seat paranormal romance. L.A. Kennedy can be found behind a mountain of books, on any given Sunday.

L.A. Kennedy's writing credits include two hit series that mix mystery, horror, paranormal romance, fantasy, and intrigue.

L.A. Kennedy loves to hear from readers. You can find her contact information, website details and author profile page at https://www.totallybound.com